B1

C000134445

P
b
b
b

EVE: HER STORY

Penelope Farmer

LONDON
VICTOR GOLLANCZ LTD
1985

First published in Great Britain 1985
by Victor Gollancz Ltd,
14 Henrietta Street, London WC2E 8QJ

British Library Cataloguing in Publication Data
Farmer, Penelope
Eve: her story.
I. Title
823'.914[F]   PR6056.A/

ISBN 0-575-03584-6

Photoset in Great Britain by
Rowland Phototypesetting Ltd,
Bury St Edmunds, Suffolk
and printed by St Edmundsbury Press
Bury St Edmunds, Suffolk

Contents

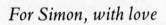

For Simon, with love

PART ONE

CHILD

Chapter One

Let me start by making this clear. I ate the fruit of the forbidden tree, the tree of knowledge, because I chose to. The serpent had nothing to do with it, even if I was pretending to tease him at first. Certainly I remember laughing as I held the fig to my lips.

I stopped laughing, I remember. But that was all. Mainly I felt disappointed. The taste of the fig seemed sweet and evasive, and I found its texture, at once fleshy and fibrous, disquieting. Besides, it was full of pips which gritted faintly on my teeth. In bite after bite, I waited for the heavens to fall—but they did not fall. There was not the smallest rumble of divine wrath; the only sound I heard was the murmur of the river beside me.

Even the serpent did not seem particularly concerned. "So now you know," he said with a faint shrug of his scaly shoulders.

"Know what?" I asked; for I'd learned nothing yet. Indeed, I knew less than I had done; all my painfully won understanding seemed to have vanished from my mind. Nor, contrary to later stories, had I grown instantly ashamed of my nakedness. (I have never been ashamed of my nakedness, and was only forced to clothe it to protect myself from the elements.) It is true that after a while when the serpent did not answer me, I wandered away and picked flowers to put in my hair, but so had I often done before. The serpent told me I was vain—then he disappeared on some business of his own in which he did not seem to want my company, and I idled the rest of the day away, trying, unsuccessfully, to forget about the matter, though once, when I extracted an errant pip from between my teeth, I caught again a hint of that unplaceable, uncomfortable and admittedly rather beguiling taste.

So things went on towards evening and the time I should meet Adam. Then I did begin wondering what to say to him; and then too, to my annoyance, found myself starting to tremble at the thought. Adam, unusually, noticed my distress at once. Observing this I told him plainly what I'd done, hoping by confession to ease myself—in vain, I merely began trembling more violently than ever. Adam did not say anything. He looked at me for a while and went away, only to reappear five minutes later carrying another fig, a slightly larger, more opulent, more purple one than mine. I hated it. It did not smell interesting, let alone beguiling, merely like something that had been left a day too long. As he took a bite he wrinkled his nose.

"Now," he said, "we shall see what we shall see."

His calmness alarmed me most of all. Neither of us referred to the garden wall which seemed now to hem us in at every turn. Nor did we mention the faint rumbles of thunder we heard from the other side. We did not say anything much, merely ate our supper without much appetite. Afterwards we went to bed and having hugged each other for a while made love, but quite differently from the way we had always done before, with a desperation which could not be assuaged and left both of us hungry, so hungry we went on till we were exhausted and were still not satisfied. I don't know how it was for Adam. But increasingly as we laboured, I had a sense of being utterly alone, his body merely an instrument by which mine attempted to seek pleasure; and found it, certainly; but then only wanted more.

In the morning, as we expected and by that time almost desired, the angels came and with self-righteous looks and gestures threw us out. There was nothing magnificent about any of them, even Michael flourishing his sword looked sly and supercilious. But there was nothing epic about Adam and me either; you'd never have guessed our fall would explain the world, at least in the serpent's version of events. Afraid, quiet, determined, we marched out into the desert, and saw before us what Lilith, Adam's first wife, my sister, my friend, had seen and feared and longed for, and made me fear and long for too, a glaring space of sand and stone and thorn bounded only by the sky itself.

We were given no time to take it in. From behind us, suddenly, came appalling screams. We turned to find all four of our guardian angels, Gabriel, Raphael, Uriel and Michael, emerging from the gate, holding the serpent high above their heads. No matter how much he kicked and writhed, no matter how unceasingly he screamed, he could not loosen their grip on him. I assumed they would set him down eventually and leave him to fend for himself in the wilderness as we would have to do. But they did not. When they had tantalised him and us enough they bore him to a flat rock and spread-eagled his body upon it—each of them pinned down one of his four limbs one-handed, while keeping their other hands free. He had fallen silent at last. His eyes flicked between them in terror and despair; stop, stop, I wanted to cry, but I too could not move or speak.

A knife appeared in each empty angelic hand. The grip of the other tightened on the serpent's limbs. Snick, snick, he was without a hand, then snick, a foot, then snick, the second hand, and snick the second foot, until he was handless and footless altogether. For the second time in my life—but now with horror and disgust—I saw raw flesh and blood. The four executioners held up the severed members triumphantly, the next moment threw them down on to the sand, while I heard behind us a padding of feet, a cacophony of growls and whines and turned to find that the animals, too, had left the garden, and in leaving it had shed their former mildness—my friends were now without exception fanged and wild-eyed. Lion and wolf, fox, jackal, leopard, dog, they leapt upon the meat and started fighting over the spoils, as if all their lives they'd known the true purpose of their claws and teeth. The serpent meanwhile was screaming again; he did not stop to draw breath, and though I covered my ears with my hands I could not shut out the sound.

The angels waited. Only when the animals had quite finished devouring the remains did they raise their knives again. This time they lopped off his genitals. Those spoils too were flung to the beasts, though the fox was quicker than the rest and ran off with most of them. Afterwards they bound his mutilated limbs to his body so tightly they fused to it. He became one length of scaly flesh which they stretched between them till it was long and narrow as a whip. Last of all they forced open his mouth, Uriel dragged out his tongue, Gabriel slit it with his knife, the screams turned to gurgles, died to a faint, despairing hiss.

Then they threw him away from them. He could only wriggle on his belly now, leaving a trail of blood behind him on the desert sand. But he had not gone far when he stopped, turned his head and looked back. His bright brown eyes were the same that I'd known in many moods, yet I had never before seen them so filled with loathing—it was directed at the angels, I thought at first. But turning my head I saw that the angels had gone, that all his hate was meant for me. It was like being pinned by a poisoned needle; the venom draining into me, I soon found myself hating and fearing him as much as he hated and feared me; as I was meant to hate and fear him. Until at last he returned to crawling painfully across the sand, and vanished beneath a rock.

And so that was that. I don't know if the angels enjoyed their task. Cruelty is a human vice, I think, not an inhuman one; and the angels are utterly inhuman, as indifferent to pain as to joy or fear or love. What they did to the serpent was what they had to do, and what they had to do was their sole desire and will. And if by it Adam and I too were cast down—well that suited them, their one quarrel with Jehovah having been our presence in the garden.

As for Jehovah. After I ate the fig he did not speak a single word. He'd sent his angels to do what was needed, and that was all. It was only when we stood alone in the wilderness, no longer able to see even the gate of Eden, that for the first and last time since our act of disobedience we heard his voice. I assume it was his voice; it sounded more like a demon's, a great cry that rebounded from horizon to horizon binding us up in it, not letting us escape—but I knew enough by then not to expect God to sound like God. Whether it was a cry of pain, triumph, loss, love, who is to say; I doubt if he could have said himself. In all events it signified that we were lost to him as he was in Eden, and that from now on we would have to attend to ourselves, because no one else was going to.

So this desert saw my second awakening to the world. And very uncomfortable it was, even more uncomfortable than the first which hadn't taken long to seem more or less delightful. But this was not delightful at all, nor ever would be by the feel of it. For the first time in my life I found myself hungry, thirsty, exhausted. My limbs and head ached unceasingly; my skin, rent by thorns and burned by sun, pricked and itched all over. It was evening already. The sun on its going down had left in place of its unpitying heat an equally unpitying chill. Adam did not seem to want to speak to me any more than I wanted to speak to him, but sat on a rock a little way away from me, his head between his hands, while I took shelter under a bush and lay curled up, trying to husband my bodily warmth.

I was not only cold and afraid but more desolate than I'd thought it possible to be, though not entirely a stranger to unhappiness; life in Eden had not always been so simple. Yet I did not find myself regretting what had happened, or feeling guilty, except on behalf of Adam and the serpent. Apart from a desperate grief, for the serpent mainly, but also for myself, I felt more angry than anything at what had been done to the three of us and the way it had been done. We'd been woken with cruel abruptness from a marvellous dream; and though I had long realised that we would have to awake some day, it did not stop me trying to recall the dream from the beginning, as if only that could soothe my present pain.

Chapter Two

In the beginning God said let there be light. And so there was light; before Eden, presumably, before us. At any rate my first awakening through Adam's wound was into light, I am quite clear about that. All I could see and feel and breathe and hear was light; it beamed from every tree and leaf, from every pore, from every cell. Light was Eden, no more, no less. And I at its heart confronted, fully grown, a world which pulsated with it; in which I saw everything and knew nothing; and in which Adam looked at me questioningly and asked "Lilith? *Lilith?*".

So the first voice I heard was Adam's, and the first word I heard was the name of Lilith, his first wife, my rival, my sister, my friend. But the first thing my eyes fell on once they had ceased being dazzled was the flesh and blood and bone of Adam's sweet, awful—significant—wound. (Just how significant of course, I did not yet know.) Even as I gazed at it in wonder it healed up entirely, concealing its secrets beneath a fine layer of skin. Soon the puckered red line that remained had also begun to fade away. And still I did not recognise what it was I saw. I did not recognise anything at all. Eden assaulted not only my eyes but each of my other senses, and how can anyone, let alone anyone new-born, take in the whole world at once?

At this moment, more or less, I heard my second voice. It was Jehovah's voice no less, addressing me as Adam's Rib and asking how I liked that. Then came other sounds, the fretting of insects, the conversations of birds, and the to and froing of a small wind in the trees around us. Jehovah asked Adam if he was pleased with me, but Adam did not seem to know. He directed at my body a blank, rather puzzled blue stare, while I, no less puzzled, was noting hand, leg, nose, mouth, eyes without any idea yet that legs were for standing and hands for making, noses for smelling, eyes for seeing, mouths for speaking and kissing and eating.

Indeed all I can truthfully say of the whole momentous occasion was that I awoke in Eden, heard Adam's voice calling Lilith's name and thereafter, but in my head, heard Jehovah's voice ordering Adam to name me; which he did obediently.

"Her name is Eve," Adam said—and that was the third name I heard. I do not know if I liked it better than Lilith or Adam. But I did know that Adam pleased me; and if I say, too, that he was a large, hairy, clumsy, rather bemused-looking man, much bigger than I was, I must add that I had nothing to compare him with, and that naturally he pleased me, since he was in a sense both my father and my mother, his flesh bounding my world as a mother's does her baby's. What else had I to cling to in this bewildering new world? The landscape—red earth, olive trees, a bird or two pecking about—was gentle enough but it did not hide me from the eye of the sun, or muffle the voice of Jehovah which kept on alternately shouting and wheedling in my head. Mighty as both were, I assumed they were one and the same, and finding Adam more comfortable to contemplate, soon put out a hand and touched him, my fingers enjoying the warmth and softness and surprising hairiness of his flesh; it was not long before he, much more warily, started touching me.

Only a little while later, the sun went down. Nothing stayed the same, it seemed, from minute to minute. This was one of the first things I learned about the world. But what I learned next was the man's unease at the gradual departure of the light, and that I did not share it. Indeed, finding the change magical, not fearful, I wasn't in the least afraid even when night came and blotted out everything. The stars in particular so enchanted me I felt almost bereft when Adam ordered a tree to stoop down, forming a bower around us, thus hiding them from my sight. He fell asleep as soon as we laid ourselves to rest. I, however, remained awake and listened to the sound of his breathing and the faint stir of leaves above my head.

Once I put out my hand to explore his body again and in doing so encountered the little flaccid thing I'd noticed between his thighs. It hardened immediately at my touch. Surprised, I took my hand away, but the sleeping Adam seized my hand and encouraged it to stroke him more while he sighed with pleasure in his sleep and I breathed in the smell of his hair and skin, the not unpleasingly acrid smell of his armpit into which I snuggled. I did not see the moon that night. Perhaps there was no moon, or perhaps I fell asleep before it rose.

Next morning when I awoke I found the sun's beams invading our bower, and Adam kneeling beside me holding out an apple.

"Eat, Eve," he said. "You must be hungry." But I did not know what he meant, so after a moment he showed me, opening his mouth and digging in his teeth, then touching my mouth to show that I should do the same. Was that the first moment I discovered I had a tongue and teeth? Perhaps it was. I found the whole thing very funny. I was laughing as I opened my mouth as wide as it would go and crammed the apple in.

I stopped laughing then. You cannot imagine what it is like to eat an apple if you have never eaten anything before. No sooner had I encountered the smoothness of its skin, than my teeth were discovering its strength—which nevertheless could not stop them breaking through to the flesh beneath. How crisp it seemed to my teeth; at the same time it melted under my tongue. Both sweet and tart, it was taste as much as texture, texture as much as taste. All I wanted sometimes was to lick it, so I did, my tongue comparing the polished skin with the cool grain of the fruit. In the end I ate every bit—its pips tasted like the almonds I had not yet tasted, while the carapace which surrounded them intrigued me by the way it caught between my teeth. When I had quite finished, Adam gave me another apple and I ate that too, more greedily this time, less reflectively. It was almost as good as the first, and afterwards I went to the stream and completed my first meal in Eden by taking my first drink out of a cup I made with my own hands, just as Adam showed me.

It was time, he said, when I had done, to introduce me to the other inhabitants of Eden. He took my hand and, having led me to a little hill overlooking a valley full of lemon trees grouped around a natural fountain, gave a shrill whistle. At once the animals started converging on us from every side. They were very orderly. They made way for each other amicably, did not push and shove, did not even fall over each other's feet, though there were so many of them and all varied in gait as well as in size and shape. Which is not to say that they were silent. The birds flying over our heads to join the rest of them were probably the noisiest, whistling and calling unceasingly, but none of the others seemed afraid to use their voices, filling the air with a roaring babble, with grunts and honks and hisses, with squeaks and coos and trills, all meant, presumably, as greetings to Adam and myself. In the end we were surrounded by fur and feather, by paw and pad and claw.

It did not occur to me to be afraid of any of them. As they came in turn to greet us I did not need to be afraid. The bear reared on his hind legs, staring at me intently with his small sad eyes. The lion padded up twitching his black-tipped tail and yawned, showing all his teeth and letting out a gust of his hot breath. The wolf did not pause, merely glanced at me sideways as he passed. The cat showed me her five kittens. The monkey swung down from the trees and chattered an involved speech of welcome. The dog licked my hands. So it went on for hours. I grew tired eventually, accepting gratefully the cow's offer of milk from her udder. She smelt earthy and wholesome, of hide and grass and just a little bit of dung. Adam watched in amazement as I sucked at a teat alongside her calf, having failed to understand either her invitation or my grateful acceptance of it. For I discovered, that morning, yet another difference between us; that I could tell what the animals were saying to me; but that Adam could not understand one word.

I cannot describe every animal I met that day, some big, some very small. But one of them I must, not least because he was so different from all the other animals, as different as Adam and I were. On his first coming towards us he reminded me of Adam a little, since he walked on two legs, like us.

He was tall and thin and sinuous, though his shoulders were

exceptionally broad. He had hands and feet like ours, except that they lacked finger and toe nails, and his skin was a pleasant tawny colour, darker than mine and Adam's, no less smooth, yet laid in layers like the scales of a fish, so fine and delicate, however, that they did not look like scales, unless peered at very closely. They formed the faintest of diamond patterns all over his body, apart from his face, where his eyes were brown and bright, pleasantly merry and sardonic but also melancholy. If his body reminded me of a man's his face did even more; which is perhaps why I liked him so much. To put it simply, my heart went out to him, and through all our quarrels and reconciliations I never took it back.

The serpent appeared to like me too; if I felt that he was trying too hard to please me, most of the animals were on that occasion. I daresay our detractors would have said that he instantly demonstrated his guile and I my fickleness. But I did not know what fickle meant, let alone how to be fickle, while he appeared much less guileful than certain other creatures who had greeted me, much less guileful than Jehovah himself, whose insidious voice inside my head was telling me what I should think about everything.

The serpent asked me how I liked the garden, I told him, confusedly, very much indeed, and how delicious the fruit was, and he said he knew where all the best varieties grew and if he could spare time from his duties one day he would give me a conducted tour, and I could gather some for myself and Adam. I was about to ask him what his duties were when he bent suddenly, and gathered from the grass at my feet a small red insect with black spots on its back which he held out, smiling wryly, saying, "Here's another one of us. I daresay you haven't met her yet, but when you do, I don't think you'll find her much of a conversationalist."

"That is just his kind of whimsy," said Lilith disapprovingly when I reported this conversation to her later. If so I didn't object to it, and don't think he meant to mock me. After seeing the gentleness, moreover, with which he transferred the small creature from his hand to mine, I liked him all the better, enough to find myself blushing in the face of his wry smile, whereupon

Adam told me sharply that there were other animals waiting to greet us.

"I know," I said, and was about to add, "But all in good time," when I noticed that the serpent had put on a new expression; a very displeased one. He bowed his head, his eyes for a moment flashed green not brown. "Wait, Adam," I said, "I still have things to say to the serpent and his friend."

"Say them another time," the serpent said. "Goodbye, Eve." And off he went, hunched slightly, looking a good deal less assured than he had a moment ago. His, "It was a pleasure to meet you," was ironic, I'm certain, though perfectly polite. I wanted to say something to soothe him, but too late, he had gone, leaving me with a memory only of his unaccountable eyes and pleasantly scaly skin, also a slight sense that I had mistreated him.

That night Adam and I ate clusters of grapes I picked from the vine, together with honey brought us by some bees, and drank fresh milk from the cow. Though few of the animals were still in sight I could hear them all around. But gradually, as the sun went down, I felt the quiet take over until only a few birds were chattering in the trees above our heads, and not long after they fell silent too.

Again Adam made a bower for us. As we lay side by side, I put my hand on the soft thing between his thighs, which he'd told me was his penis; even as I touched it it grew hard once more, growing still harder as I stroked it, and still hotter. Adam began sighing. At last he pushed my hand away and raising himself on one elbow looked down at me lying on our grassy bed. He laid a finger against his lips and licked it. Slowly, slowly, he drew it across each of my breasts in turn, while I lay holding my breath and waiting for I knew not what, without apprehension, for what did I have to fear? Suddenly Adam rolled over and lay on top of me, kissing my mouth gently. Feeling his organ stiff against my thighs, I opened them willingly, though not knowing why I should need to, since I had little idea of what lay between them. But Adam seemed to. His flesh probed and probed, and my flesh too knew its nature well enough, opening before him very neatly

21

and comfortably, till to my surprise and delight it gave way entirely, and his organ continuing to ride deeper and deeper, allowed it to bury itself altogether and we were joined as one.

I remember thinking: this is how it is; we have been completed now, and so, complete, we will inhabit the garden. I felt utterly content. As Adam moved in me with increasing speed and urgency I began moving with him, arching myself against him in perfect unison. And when he began shuddering I shuddered too, his pleasure gliding in me more sweetly than the honey, warmer and richer than the milk we had drunk from the cow. And afterwards, for a while, we lay together quietly, joined still, though his organ was gentle inside me. Yet I was not disappointed when we separated, not even surprised. That too was how it was. No questions waited to be asked. Not a single question needed to be answered. My body and my mind alike—I could no longer tell one from the other—lay glowing and easy, and I slid into sleep as simply as Adam had, who lay breathing evenly beside me.

Chapter Three

During my first days in Eden I did not encounter the serpent again. I did not encounter anyone, but was left to wander the garden with the animals, sometimes in Adam's company, sometimes by myself. How Adam occupied himself on those days he left me to myself, I neither knew nor cared. I was not lonely in the least; how could I be in such a place with so much to amuse and delight me?

All day I would wander, from hill to hill, from valley to valley, discovering each time a different landscape more beautiful than the last—every landscape in the world was to be found in Eden. In any one I chose I could spend a minute, an hour, a week, as long as I wanted: on a plain of grass set with flowering trees, reaching away in all directions; beneath a grove of olive trees, anemones growing underfoot; on a bare southern slope, like the one on which I first awoke, where at every step I crushed wild marjoram and thyme; in summer gardens scented with lilies and pinks; among rolling hills and valleys, the folds of which, as Adam pointed out to me teasingly, resembled the shape of my own body, having breasts and thighs and little secret clefts between them. "I made them to celebrate you, Eve," he told me, but I did not understand what he meant, and though I liked answers from the beginning, had not yet learned what questions to ask.

Jehovah spoke to me often as I wandered. For the moment, however, he had quietened his voice—perhaps he realised how he'd confused me at the start. Now he soothed, cooed, reassured, like my father and my mother. Also he flattered me, and that was something different again. I was too innocent—or

ignorant—to recognise what he was doing, and responded precisely as I'm sure he wanted me to, very coyly and with a girlish
flirtatiousness it embarrasses me to remember; particularly as I
also seem to remember imagining he was in my power and not
the other way about. How could I not imagine such a thing when
every feature in the landscape appeared designed for my delight,
when the wish of all creatures was apparently to please me?

Adam especially seemed to wish to please me; I, in my turn,
believed I loved him very much. Each evening I would bring a
gift, a fruit or flower or stone, and he would have some stranger
gift for me: curiously fretted seeds, for instance, from fruit I'd
never seen; a feather from a brilliant bird; a green-veined stone
he'd polished very highly. Once he brought a pipe cut out of a
reed on which he taught me to play a haunting tune. Another day
he handed me five small brown stones. I looked at them in
bewilderment, until he showed me how to throw them up in the
air in ones or twos, or even, as we grew more skilful, five at a
time, and catch them on the backs of our hands. On still another
occasion he brought me a sea-shell; if I did not yet know that the
sea existed, the shape and smell of this curiously fluted thing
so intrigued me, I held and sniffed at it for a particularly long
time.

My life altogether pleasant and good, I hardly noticed how
rarely Adam passed the day at my side. Though I still had not met
the serpent again, and already regretted it, the company of the
animals kept me from being lonely. Increasingly, too, I grew
aware of other presences in the garden. Walking along an avenue
of trees, for instance, I'd fancy someone was moving ahead of
me, slowly it seemed, yet I could never catch up. Or maybe,
breasting a hillside, a figure would be standing directly in my
path. I'd stop immediately and then find no one there. Most
frequent and most teasing were distant energetic forms that on
closer acquaintance turned out to be trees or rocks. It made me
wonder sometimes if the whole garden was not alive and animal.

None of this much worried or even puzzled me for long. If I
was conscious that many mysteries remained, I saw no need to sit
and brood on them; not, that is, until the day I met the archangel

Michael in an orchard of comfortable and aged-looking apple and pear trees, covered in ripe fruit. One of them, a pear tree I thought, turned out to be Michael himself. I saw his eyes move first, then he stepped forward to meet me. Though his body did not fill the space between the trees I could not have got past him had I wanted to. But I did not want to.

The main reason I felt uneasy, I think, was because I did not know where to place him. He did not look like an animal, more like Adam, if anything; yet certainly he was not a man. For a second's terror and excitement I thought Jehovah had made himself visible at last. Meanwhile, as I stared at him, he stared back at me, without appearing to move one single muscle—even his eyes were still as stone. After a few minutes a fly came and settled on his face, paused briefly at the corner of his mouth, marched right to left along his lower lip, paraded under his left eye, from left to right this time, sipped delicately from the corner, sat up and having cleaned its forefeet, raised its wings and flew away.

"Doesn't it tickle?" I asked. But Michael remained as motionless as ever, and I received no answer. The blankness of his look so terrified me suddenly, that I blurted out, "Who are you? Who are you?"

Michael gave a faint and indifferent smile. "I am Michael, archangel of the Lord," he intoned rather than said. And when I still looked baffled he went on, "I am God's servant just as you are God's servant."

"Am I?" I asked, my panic subsiding a little. "He never told me. Not in so many words."

"He should not have needed to tell you," Michael chided me. "You should know in every portion of your flesh that your function and duty is to adore the Lord our God, blessed be his name, and observe his righteousness."

I had never heard such phrases before. They sounded so funny that I laughed out loud. Though Michael still looked at me indifferently, clearly he was not pleased.

"The Lord's name may not be taken in vain or mocked," he chanted.

25

"Now you have told me my duties, will you tell me yours?" I said meekly. "Mind out, you're about to step on a rotten pear."

Michael stepped on the pear anyway and crushed it. I smelled its sweet, decaying, yet not uninviting scent rise up from under his unsullied feet. I wish I could describe exactly how he looked. But if I shut my eyes all I can see—and smell—and hear—is the pear tree in the orchard where I met him. (The tree was full of wasps to judge by its buzzing. Soon one came and sat on Michael's cheek and remained there throughout the rest of our conversation. His face did not acknowledge its presence either, any more than it had acknowledged the presence of the fly.) All I can report is how Michael told me that he too had only to adore the Lord and obey his commandments.

One commandment, it appeared, was to watch over Adam and myself. I did not altogether like the sound of that. But when I protested he proclaimed, relentlessly, "God's commandments are not to be questioned, God forbid. The Lord is righteous. Obedience to him is praise." Which led to me complaining, helplessly, that Michael kept on using words I did not understand: what did righteousness mean, for example. And what about obedience? Michael gave, I remember, a most peculiar smile, his first visible reaction to anything I had said.

"The nature of righteousness is something you will learn with the nature of obedience; and you will not find the learning easy."

I felt desperate suddenly; I demanded, defiantly, "And what if I don't *want* to learn?"

Michael looked at me in silence for a moment, his eyes brighter and colder than ever; I fancy they were green as glass. His voice flowed out like bitter juice.

"But you will learn. In this you will have no choice, as most of us have no choice in anything."

"I don't like you, I don't like you," I cried out helplessly, the certainty dragged from my mouth, before I knew it with my understanding.

"Fortunately," said Michael, "that is immaterial. There is no need for you to like me. Or I you; God forbid."

"But I haven't done you any harm," I argued. "Have I?"

"Haven't you?" replied Michael. "Why don't you ask the man whom God made in his image? Why don't you ask the mighty namer of the animals? You know, of course, that Adam gave the animals their names?"

"He said something about it, I did not take much notice."

"And perhaps he never told you how he was able to name them? Perhaps he never told you he stole the names from one of us."

"From *us*? Are there more of you? *Angels*," I said, appalled.

"Of course he never told you that, either? Never mentioned angels, archangels, seraphim, cherubim, princedoms, powers, God's first servants, created in glory? Oh no, Adam would never tell you about us, God forbid," replied Michael in an acid torrent yet still retaining his unutterable indifference, as if in the end even his own pain was of no importance to him. I cannot describe it; any more than I can describe the mixture of worship and loathing with which he proceeded to relate how Jehovah had contrived through Adam to cheat the angels of their due. First he'd proclaimed that whichever of his creation named the animals would be bowed down to by the rest, then he'd erased the names from the mind of Sammael, the leader of the angels, and put them into the mind of Adam. Nor had Adam demurred; taking the gift as his due, he'd named the animals directly, making it seem that the names came straight out of his own head.

The angel Sammael, Michael went on to tell me, had defied Jehovah thereafter and still refused to bow down to Adam with all the other angels. He had been cast out of paradise for his disobedience, quite unfairly, I thought; indeed I found the whole story shocking. I did not, however, say so in the face of Michael's disdain. Through him, I think, I felt real fear for the first time, not the holy terror imposed on me by God in the beginning, but the kind of mean, all-pervasive fear you can never quite pin down. My fear increased when Michael began to sing. In his voice was neither maturity nor emotion, just a chilly purity, like a star illuminating nothing but itself. "Holy, holy, holy," it went. "Holy, holy, holy." It seemed there could never be any end it continued so relentlessly, long after Michael had faded from my sight.

I found myself screaming inside my head, "Oh God. Oh God."

Of course Jehovah came at once. He never could resist such appeals. Yet he would not listen to what I had to say, brushing aside my indignation as if it were some charming whim. And when I persisted he told me it was none of my business, a weight behind his voice that took my breath away and that I dared not dispute. It left me feeling depressed, much too depressed to banter with him as usual. Indeed the banter merely seemed foolish, and I began to hate the voice inside my head so obviously that Jehovah told me I was delightful when I scowled, in a parody of his usual avuncular manner clearly meant to be annoying. Then his presence vanished from my head laughing as it did so, but leaving me more afraid than ever. Why did he need such hate—not mine, the angels'? Why did he need such frigid adoration?

It was evening now. I went off to find Adam, hoping he at least would understand my fears, and confirm my indignation. If he'd told me that he'd had no choice but to name the animals, that it had not been possible to resist God's will, I would have understood that; all I wanted was some sign of pity for the angels. But I was wrong in assuming he must pity them for what had happened. Having heard me out he only shrugged and when I persisted with my story he grew angry. Though it did not take long to soothe him, though soon we lay in each other's arms as usual, it was not enough; I felt abandoned, even a little betrayed.

That night, for some reason, I kept remembering the serpent. Indeed as Adam slept I found myself so longing to meet him I determined to call his name next time I went walking in the garden, and ask him what he thought about the matter.

But, still, it seemed, I was not to meet the serpent. First I had to meet my sister: Lilith.

Chapter Four

One evening it was raining in Eden. I thought this new sensation delightful. The harder the rain fell the more joyfully I ran, letting the water course over my body, opening my mouth to catch its drops upon my tongue.

We slept dry all night in one of Adam's bowers. I could hear the rain clattering on the leaves above our heads, but when I awoke next morning it had stopped, though the whole world smelled of it. I had never smelled wet earth before. It seemed very clean and plain after the heady sweetness of the blossoms. I liked it. I liked the way in which the rain had transformed the garden. It was not simply that everything was wet—the sodden earth a darker red, each leaf and blade hung with water drops—it seemed to have driven the plants into such furious growth. The grass was twice as high, foliage much thicker. Clear paths I had walked on yesterday were almost obliterated and thick with mud, which oozed rather pleasantly between my toes.

As I went on, moving ever more slowly, the green advanced inexorably; I had to push my way through it. The air grew warmer and wetter; I found myself walking in a deep forest, among trees whose leaves were like blades and fans and fronds, while their trunks and branches were hung with creepers bearing flowers as vivid in colour as their scents were pervasive.

I had never seen the garden as rampant as this. The plants might have been growing before my very eyes. At the same time I smelled an ever stronger, rotting smell, and all at once emerged into a clearing almost filled by a large pond, round which trees and plants and creepers crowded. The water in places reflected them. Not knowing about reflections, I assumed that the same kinds of trees and plants and creepers must also grow beneath the water. There were certainly flowers growing on top of it, their blossoms wide and stiffly petalled, their round leaves flat against the surface. Below them I saw fishes darting, above hovered purple dragonflies with transparent wings. Brilliant birds hiding among the brilliant blossoms of the trees and bushes added their voices to the hum of insects, the plash of water, the creakings and sighings from the forest behind me. It was a noisy and crowded world in which I met Lilith for the first time.

I met myself first, however. The sun disappeared behind a cloud and suddenly a face stared up at me from the water; a face like Adam's only it was not Adam's, pale, glimmering, with the weeds swaying through it. As the sky darkened it grew still clearer and in my puzzlement and delight I put one hand to my lips. Immediately a hand went to the lips of the face in the water also. When I knelt down and leaned out over the pond, the face moved as I moved mine, and below it I saw two breasts with nipples, just like mine.

I don't know at what point I realised they were mine. Maybe not till I saw the two faces reflected. Yet I was not surprised to see a second face. I'd begun braiding my hair at the time, perhaps I'd thought of going into the water to meet my image which, as I expected by now, was braiding its hair too. When the other one appeared behind it, smiling, I assumed only that the reflection had doubled. Then the sun went behind a cloud again and I saw how different it was to the other, with its dark eyes and wild hair. In my sudden bewilderment I stopped smiling. My reflected image stopped smiling too, but not the new one, it smiled more broadly than ever, then suddenly screwed itself up. When the sneeze came from behind me I spun round with a cry, and found her standing there. Lilith. *Lilith*.

Would I have recognised her as a woman, I wonder, if I had not just seen the shape of my own body? Would I have thought her another angel? Who knows. The fact was I saw her as a sister instantly, and with unutterable joy, as if I'd longed for her always without knowing that I had.

The way she stared, meanwhile, she might have been surprised to see me. But I do not think she was.

"Who are you?" was all that I could say.

"*You're* Eve," she said.

"How did you know?" I asked suspiciously, feeling she was laughing at me, though her expression remained grave.

"All names are known in Eden," said Lilith portentously, gave another small sneeze, then burst out laughing. Unable to see the joke I felt both confused and hurt, a mixture of sensations with which I grew well-acquainted as I got to know Lilith better.

"But I do not know yours," I replied in an offended voice.

"But I think you do. I am Lilith."

"I've never heard of you," I stated righteously. She burst out laughing again, and said, "Oh Eve, if you could but see your face."

I turned my back on her and stirred the water with my foot. Because her name did stir up some memory after all, I did not know what. I did not even want to know, the memory made me uneasy, and I could not tell why. All I wanted—despite the mockery, and against my own intentions—was to look at her. Maybe she realised it. I turned, simultaneously she turned towards me, staring at me with her lips slightly parted just as I stared at her. Again we might have been reflections of each other.

How familiar her body was, at the same time how unfamiliar. Mine was sturdier, I think, and several inches taller—it seemed odd to look down on her after always looking up at Adam. Nonetheless her flesh was much more rounded than my flesh, her breasts as firm as apples, while below her narrow waist her hips and thighs swelled voluptuously. Between them stood a triangle of hair like my own, except that hers was reddish-black and less curly than mine. Yet the hair that sprang wildly from her head was much curlier and flowed down almost to her small feet, which she had planted so firmly on the jungle floor she might have grown there, like the other plants.

Of all the jungle flowers, however, she was the most exotic and brilliant; with her brown eyes that gazed at me so intently; with her arched brows and deep lids she lowered now and then as if to protect her eyes from my equally intent gaze; with her nose slightly pink from sneezing, and her mouth fine-drawn and twitching in amusement or impatience, it was hard to tell which.

I thought she was beautiful. At the same time, I felt afraid of her, afraid as I'd been of Michael, only in a different way. Once I found myself wanting to scream out. Go away, go away. But of course I did not. I did not dare. I knew she would simply have laughed at me and stayed where she was. Also, despite my doubt and fear, I had a huge longing to lay my head upon her breast; the longing of a daughter for a mother.

In the end I could not resist it. I reached out my hand; but before it met its goal Lilith gave a little giggle, tossed her head sharply as if she knew exactly what I was after and did not want it in the least, dug her fingers into my skin and simultaneously pushed me away. I stumbled backwards—I would have landed in the pool, I think, but for Lilith yanking me towards her no less fiercely than she had just pushed me away. For an instant as we clung to each other in order to steady ourselves I felt her springy hair brush my skin—then we stood apart, Lilith brushing at herself so energetically she might have been trying to rid herself of a contagion.

"How you do stare at me, Eve," she said coolly.

"I'm sorry," I said, casting my head down in embarrassment. It did not occur to me till afterwards that she had stared fully as hard at me.

"Have you never seen another woman?" she asked. "No, of course not. How could you? For that matter I never saw another woman either. How clever of me to recognise you, don't you think, Eve?" She laughed and laughed. I felt confused all over again and resentful besides. I did not see why I should reply to her.

"Can't you speak?" enquired Lilith. "Have you nothing to say?"

My annoyance gave me courage. "What are you doing here?" I asked. "Where do you come from? God told us the garden was ours alone."

"How inquisitive you are," returned Lilith, her voice light but definitely sharper.

"What are you doing here?" I persisted obstinately.

"I'm not obliged to answer any questions," Lilith said, but less severely. Then she put out her hand and touched my hair, adding, "Don't scowl, Eve. And don't let's quarrel. Can you not see how glad I am to have met another woman? I really do like you. I really do. And besides, when you're not scowling you are so very pretty."

I hardly dared register the longing in her voice, let alone the longing I also felt, though I did not understand where it came from, any more than I understood the sudden wave of sympathy that rose between us out of nothing.

"You're not the least like Adam," I said, confusedly.

"I should hope not," she replied, then gave another peal of laughter and the moment was past. For immediately she started sneezing again violently, turned away to collect herself and when she turned back added, "It's getting late." (And indeed it was, though we seemed to have been together such a little time—the sky was beginning to grow pink and the shadows in the forest deeper and deeper.) "Isn't it time you were going home to your companion?"

"But what of you? Where will you go? Do you want to come with me?" I asked.

"I have my haunts," said Lilith. "I don't need yours."

"But you're alone?"

"If I choose to be."

Thus warned, I did not press the matter any further, asked instead, "Will I see you again?"

"Maybe. If I want. I shall go now, Eve, goodnight."

She looked at me for a moment uncertainly, before leaning forward, and with a small, still uncertain smile kissing me coolly on the lips. "Goodbye," she said, and sneezed for the last time in my presence once, twice, three times.

Then she was gone. The meeting scarcely seemed to have been at all. "Come back," I cried. "Come back," but my words echoed across the water unanswered. The flowers glowing still more brightly in the growing dusk, all that came back were sneezes, and I might have imagined even them.

I heard startled birds rising and chattering loudly. Twigs cracked between the trees, something broke on the surface of the pond. As I stood touching myself very gently there were bubbles and quivering circles and a slightly sulphurous but not entirely unpleasant smell. I touched my breasts; I touched my belly and triangle of hair. For the first time I reached below them and explored the place between my thighs that only Adam's penis had known till now. I ran a finger inside the lips I found and put it to my other lips, and tasted, also for the first time, my own salty taste and smelled my strange, deep smell. I was not wholly sure if I liked it, any more than I was sure if I wholly liked Lilith. She not only made me feel nervous, I did not think I could ever learn to keep up with the way she talked.

And now I must interrupt my story briefly. Having let myself regain for a while the sweet scents of Eden I'm tempted to forget the harsher odours of the desert. Yet if I do, if I leave them out of my tale, I risk making it seem that eating the fig was a mere act of defiance, instead of the one that both proclaimed and made me a woman.

Of course I did not see it at that time, after we'd been thrown out of the garden; much of what I'd learned had been wiped, for the moment, from my mind. Eyeing in horror the empty landscape reaching away, I saw only how little I knew and understood; was very soon to learn how little in particular I knew and understood my husband, despite the life that we had shared.

Neither of us could understand, for instance, why the other had eaten the forbidden fruit. Adam seemed to view both my action, and my attempts to explain it as totally frivolous. Yet all he would say as to his own motives was, "I'd lost one wife. I was determined not to lose another." Since he never told me, merely left me to infer it, I did not immediately realise that he meant he loved me, and that given a choice between his wife and Eden he'd had no choice but to leave Eden too. Nor did I remember then, at that moment, that he would not have done the same thing for his first wife Lilith; because Jehovah had not opened his flesh on her account.

34

Apart from which, I did not understand Adam's reaction to the serpent's fate, any more than he could understand mine. I grieved for the serpent unceasingly in those early days, when I wasn't grieving for Eden and myself; after a while it swallowed up my other griefs, and came to stand for them. Adam too grieved deeply for what we had lost, but he used the serpent's fate as the focus of his anger, against me, the desert, the God he thought he ought to love. The serpent, he said viciously, deserved all he got, the slimy wretch; he'd always said he wasn't to be trusted, he'd always told me not to spend so much time with him. Once or twice when I was stupid enough to tell him I was weeping for the serpent he flew into a great rage about it—such a rage that he seemed insane.

But we barely exchanged words on any subject these days, beyond what was necessary for simple survival. Above everything else, therefore, we were lonely. Jehovah did not speak to us of course, and though we could hear the animals by night and day, our former friends now hid from us in fear. As for the angels—in those days, I think, we even missed the angels; it was impossible to believe they existed any more. Perhaps I found the pain slightly easier to bear, since I could ease some of my wretchedness by shouting and weeping, but Adam didn't seem to know how to weep. Indeed after a while he no longer knew how to be angry either, but would sit each evening some way away from me, his head between his hands, gazing at the ground just as on our first evening. At night, we still slept close to one another, but that was because we knew no other way to keep warm, and often shivered so much even then that neither of us slept all night.

By day, of course, ripe fruits no longer falling to our hands, we were chained helplessly, like animals, to the struggle to survive. For struggle we did, constantly, unendingly, against cruel weather and an equally cruel land, against heat, cold, wind and sometimes even rain. Jehovah clearly meant us to survive. But equally clearly he intended life to be hard for us. The water we sought for so painfully was brackish more often than not; the fruits were sour and withered. Sometimes I found them and brought them to Adam, and got no thanks for it. On other days he fed me, and I wasn't grateful either, though those handfuls of bitter berries, all we would have to show for a long day's gleaning under the burning sun, were infinitely more precious than a huge cluster reached down from a branch in Eden. But at the time I did not want life. Indeed only the blindest of instincts kept me moving on, my body daily more skeletal, my hair matted, my skin scratched and grazed all over and thick with dust and dirt.

I can remember still the lowest point of my despair; it was the day I began to bleed. Having no means of knowing that such loss of perfection meant that out here in the desert I'd become a woman at last, I assumed it was Jehovah's final punishment, that I too like the serpent had been mutilated. The most terrifying thing was how hot the blood felt as it coursed from my womb, staining the earth and some desert plant beneath me, a succulent little thing with fleshy tendrils on which it gleamed ominously red in the early evening sun. No matter what I did I couldn't staunch the flow, though I tried desperately to do so, even stuffing my fingers inside myself as I wept with shame and terror.

If shame determined me to avoid Adam that evening, terror drove me to him in the end. But he only looked appalled and thereafter blank, saying with a shrug, "I'm sorry, Eve, but what can I do about it? I daresay it's yet another sign of God's wrath that we brought upon ourselves." Since that was just what I feared I merely howled the louder, and ran away from him and flung myself down upon the earth and ground my face into it. Yet again, amid my wretchedness, grief for the serpent was uppermost. He would have comforted me, I thought, he would have reassured me. For the first time I lay alone all night, feeling the warm blood trickling from my body, letting myself be overcome by self-pity among more fundamental griefs, enraged among other things that the serpent had let himself be so treated and hence abandoned me.

A week after it had started my bleeding eased, more or less. And a week after that I met Sammael the fallen angel of Michael's story. Who had without doubt chosen his moment very carefully. The act that followed wasn't exactly an act of love. He, you could say, was taking his revenge on mankind on the one hand and on Jehovah on the other for what had been done to him when he refused to bow down to Adam. But let me point out that I too was avenging myself and with me my former friend the serpent; that in this matter, at least, Sammael and I conspired to exorcise our mutual pain and grief. I knew it was so, even as he threw me to the ground and took me from behind, his rod burning piti-lessly inside me, even as I screamed aloud with anger and relief, my nose and mouth pressed into the sand so that I could scarcely breathe.

Indeed, though it was only because of the serpent, I'm glad to this day that Cain was not entirely conceived in hate. Maybe it was for that reason Sammael's seed clung to my womb as persistently as the hooks of the desert burrs clung to my hair and flesh. Maybe, even in my misery, I was beginning to loathe the desert less.

Adam had arrived almost at once, in time, I think, to see Sammael depart; certainly in time to find me lying there, my legs thrown out, my arms cradling my head. If I'd leapt to my feet immediately and appeared contrite or at the very least disturbed by what had happened, he might perhaps have forgiven me. But by now I was feeling such release and even pleasure—since we came to the desert Adam had not once reached out to me in love—that all I could do was lie blinking up at him, slowly and lazily stretching every limb.

"Whore," he said wearily. "Dirty whore."

I don't think I had noticed before how utterly weary he had grown. His eyes were heavy with exhaustion, his shoulders hunched, his flesh shrunk back on to his bones; there were even some grey hairs in his beard and hair. What I saw in him besides, of course, were the signs of ageing, but I did not recognise them as such any more than I had recognised similar signs in Lilith. How could I? In Eden men and animals did not age.

Thus my languor gave way rapidly to pity as I gazed at him. But still I could not find the strength to move. And in the end he gave one simple, weary shrug and walked away between the dunes and the thorn bushes. When at last I struggled to my feet there was no sign of him. I ran and shouted but he did not appear—in any case night was coming on fast, though I went on calling long after it was too dark to see where I was going, let alone catch any movement in the surrounding wilderness. Only towards midnight did I give up and fling myself down again to weep until I could weep no more. My tears were as much for him as for myself. His life in the desert would be much more precarious than mine, the serpent having not taught him any of his skills.

Chapter Five

So I return to Eden, to our wedding day; a day managed by Jehovah from beginning to end for his own purposes. In all senses that mattered, Adam and I were already husband and wife; what need, then, did we have of a wedding day? So Lilith asked on being told of it; adding, much later, that she and Adam had never had one. Maybe, on his second attempt, Jehovah saw it as a means of binding his creation. Certainly, when he woke us with the announcement of what was in store, neither Adam nor I knew what he was talking about. Rather sleepily and reluctantly we roused ourselves, and tumbled out into a landscape and season so lush it was intended, obviously, to sweep our sense away.

There was full new foliage, I remember, and springing grass, and an insect hum as persistent as the song of the birds. Over everything hung a lascivious reek which played on skin and nose alike, the sun in drying out all the luscious juices creating a vapour so fine it invaded every pore of our flesh.

Adam recoiled a little at the bombardment. I, however, exulted, throwing back my head and snuffing up the scents no less greedily than my ears responded to the music of birds and insects and my eyes to the vibrancy of green and blue and yellow. I was too absorbed to notice Adam led away by invisible hands, let alone to notice the shimmer of light on distant hills, the first warning, perhaps, in that day full of blessings and warnings. I felt simply that the whole of creation was celebrating me, and I responded in the only way I could by celebrating it.

But I was not left to celebrate for long. Somewhat to my dismay after my encounter with Michael, Jehovah summoned two angels to attend me. I thought one of them was Michael, till I saw he had eyes of fire, not ice. I could make no such mistake about the other one; though he hooded his eyes, he greeted me much too amiably to be Michael, announcing himself as Raphael and his fellow as Gabriel. They had brought me my breakfast, he went on—would I be pleased to eat? Strange and delectable fruits that I've seen in no place since were heaped on a shining platter; sweet wine was brimming in a golden cup.

Afterwards when Raphael, bowing, had removed the dish, Jehovah instructed me to rise to my feet. Immediately I felt soft hands being laid upon my neck. They were not the angels' hands I felt. I never did feel the angels' hands, yet their touch would have been icy, I am sure—and maybe, even, I should not have survived it. These hands, though invisible, were warm as they lifted my hair gently from my neck and brushed it smooth. Thereafter deft fingers separated the strands, plaited them intricately and fastened them up upon my head. My eyes were blazing gems besides, my mouth full of pearls, my nipples like roses; between my thighs stood the triangle of burnished hair.

It is not conceit which makes me describe myself like this— though I see no reason why I should not rejoice in my beauty when it's appropriate to do so. I am merely repeating Jehovah's descriptions of my body as pronounced to the angels, my sulky attendants. I think he meant to annoy them—clearly they hated every word of it. Raphael attempted a twisted smile or two, Gabriel's eyes blazed dangerously. Yet for all that they opened their mouths very dutifully and sang hearty praises to each part of my body in turn, while Jehovah himself, like a mother, clothed me in my own nakedness, touching me with such tenderness before, behind, between, I melted as to a mother and laid my head as if upon his breast. He took his hands away at last. I heard a sigh behind me of contentment—simultaneously the birds and angels stopped their voices, and I sighed my own pleasure into silence.

We found my bridegroom waiting, surrounded by animals, beneath a grove of spreading trees whose branches set with huge, waxy blossoms made our wedding canopy. In a day full of unheeded warnings I do not remember the ceremony that followed offering us any in particular, unlike the ceremonies of weddings since Eden. Adam, for instance, was given no ring to bind me. Nor did he break any vessel beneath his feet. Nor did our congregation wish us good luck, why should they have, all Eden was good luck?

Yet I remember that at the point in the ceremony at which in these sadder and wiser days a glass would have been broken, two birds began to fight in the trees above our heads. We could not see them in the dense foliage. The first we knew of it was a sudden squawk and scuffle, followed by a violent shaking of the waxy pink blooms. It quietened in a moment, no doubt out of respect for the occasion, but a moment later, as Adam and I stood waiting for Jehovah to pronounce his final blessing, a succession of small feathers came floating gently down. One of them landed on Adam's shoulder. I picked it off lovingly and held it in my hand throughout the sermon that followed.

It began harmlessly enough, this ominous discourse. I, according to Jehovah, was to be the flint to Adam's fire, the clapper to his never silent bell; he both my lion and my dove and the kernel of every fruit I enjoyed in Eden. I thought it sounded pretty but meaningless and had almost given up listening when suddenly Jehovah's tone changed completely; we'd ignore, he said, at our peril, what he had to tell us now.

So it was we learned, for the first time, of the two trees standing at the heart of Eden, the trees of life and knowledge; learned too that though we might eat freely from the one, from the other, the tree of knowledge, we might not, except on pain of the most bitter penalty. What that penalty was Jehovah did not say. Having promised to show us the trees in the cool of the evening, he pronounced a last and particularly sonorous blessing, while we meekly and gladly bowed our heads, and shifted feet aching from standing still so long.

Not until the voice fell silent did I notice the four angels standing at each corner of our flowering canopy, Michael, Gabriel, Raphael and a fourth with a sour expression whose name I learned later was Uriel. For a moment they spread their wings enclosing us, each one smiling implacably with hot eyes or cold, and in that time only they withstood all bullying; Jehovah himself could not hurt them in any way at all. Briefly I felt that danger, just as I had felt all the other ones. But there was nothing I could do about it, and the next minute I had forgotten the whole affair.

Later the angels brought us our wedding feast, more fruits of almost every kind and sweet intoxicating liquors. They were so polite and attentive I had the feeling they were overdoing it; I would have choked had I accepted all the sweet things with which they plied us. Even so I downed cupful after cupful of wine, feeling my cheeks grow red, my hair become increasingly dishevelled. Soon I no longer cared that Uriel was sneering at me, Michael smiling sarcastically, Gabriel wearing an expression of furious disdain. Only Raphael's look was at all ambiguous, somewhere between contempt and servility and pity.

Adam, my husband, appeared equally oblivious of warnings. Free for once from his usual clumsiness, he gazed lovingly into my eyes, laughing tenderly at my silliest remarks instead of looking at me as he usually did, as if he was only half-listening. Presently, drugged with wine and fruit, we fell asleep in each other's arms. When we awoke under the flowering tree beneath which we'd placed ourselves, we found all the animals crowding around us.

A donkey had laid his head upon one of my shoulders; a voluptuous bird was nestling on the other; a goat insisted on my embracing him; a cat lay, purring loudly upon my lap. As for Adam his face was being licked very lovingly by two dogs and a fox; a jackdaw and a magpie were nibbling each of his ears, while a determined sheep had made him a backrest (when we went to bed that night his back was still greasy and smelled faintly of her pleasantly rancid wool).

There was no sign of Jehovah, though I daresay he watched this happy scene with satisfied benevolence as long as it suited him. It was not for very long. Still a little tipsy perhaps, I hardly noticed when the animals melted away—but suddenly the sun was beginning to go down and we were quite alone, except for the voice of Jehovah bidding us to follow it to the trees of life and knowledge. I had almost forgotten his sermon by that time. It took me a moment or two to know what Jehovah meant.

Thus it was towards sunset on our wedding day we saw the trees at last—and what can I say about them? They did not much impress me. One of them was covered in blossom, it is true, but neither bore any fruit; the question of our eating it was meaningless as yet. On the other hand I liked the place where the trees stood, on an island surrounded by a river clear as crystal which looped round their very roots and across which we had to wade to reach them. One a fig tree, the other an apple, they were perhaps a little taller than most fruit trees in the garden, otherwise they looked no different.

The fig, especially, was disappointing. Though its trunk swelled as voluptuously as the body of a woman, though there were leaves already on its pallid branches, it held nothing else but some small green nodules that had no smell when I put my nose to them. (The apple blossom had no smell either, but it was very much prettier.)

Adam looked anxious. "I don't think you should even touch those trees," he said. But Jehovah laughed, and told him I could touch them as much as I liked, it was only the fruit I must not eat; the apples not till it was time; the figs not at all, not ever.

"And if I did?" I asked him, idly. And was told in a quiet voice I'd bring death upon my husband and myself.

"What's death?" I asked. And when I got no answer, repeated my question; "Death, what's that?" Even as I did so I felt Jehovah melt away. Adam meanwhile was shaking his head at me; to tease him I went on chanting for a little while, death, death, death. But I could only lay such weight on that word as God had when he spoke it. And he hadn't laid any weight there; indeed he made the sound so lightly I could not imagine fearing it and ceased very quickly to wonder what it meant.

And if on our way to sleep I saw a shadow move in the distance, I thought nothing of that either. I was exhausted suddenly. In any case I believed it was an angel, though lacking their edge of light. Adam did not seem to have noticed. Perhaps he would have recognised the shadow if he had, the Sammael of Michael's story, no stranger to him as he still was to me. It did not matter very much. The last warning of the day meant no more than the first. Falling asleep contentedly in my husband's arms I dreamed only of the blessings.

Chapter Six

I've said how elusive the serpent was before my wedding day;
until that time I only saw him once, during my first meeting with
the animals. At the wedding there was no sign of his lithe form.
Thereafter the situation reversed itself; I came across him
wherever I went.

The very next morning, not long after Adam had departed on
his still-mysterious business, I was wandering in a grove of
orange trees when I heard a noise above my head and looked up to
find the serpent perched in one of them, wielding an object quite
unlike anything I'd ever seen before. Though he nodded at me
and smiled faintly, he did not seem the least interested in my
presence. He just went on with his work, while I watched,
curiously, ducking out of the way every now and then because of
the twigs, leaves and even small branches that came tumbling
down.

Having found him at last I was determined not to let him go.
But almost a whole morning had passed before my patience was
rewarded, and by then I'd decided, angrily, that he was deliberately annoying me. Quite likely he was; it also has to be said that I
was not used to being ignored on account of someone's work. At
the same time I had grown increasingly intrigued by what the
serpent was doing, in particular by the little flash and gleam of the
mysterious instrument he was wielding, with its power to sever
at a single stroke the shiny foliage of the orange tree.

But when he slid down at last and landed at my side, very
careful not to touch me, I noticed, as he brushed dust off himself,
the strange instrument was not in evidence. All he carried was a
bag made of fibres interwoven and knotted together, containing

several oranges which he must have picked from the tree as he worked.

I found him no less intriguing than I had at our first encounter. The smell of the oranges around us seemed to emanate not only from the trees but from his body. His eyes having little gold glints in them, as if they too reflected the fruit, the hint of scales on his cheeks so pleasant and unusual, I could not go on being annoyed with him for long.

He became easier too as we emerged into the sunlight from the shade of the trees. Whereas before he would not look at me, now he did not take his eyes away, and it was I who began to feel embarrassed.

"How lovely you look, Eve," he said after a while. "What a shame I missed your marriage yesterday—I really would have liked to congratulate you both."

I glanced at him suspiciously, but he looked honest enough, even bashful, passing his bag of oranges from hand to hand—it reminded me for some reason, the thought touched me a little, that he was the only animal in the garden who did not appear to have a mate.

He saw me looking at his bag. With a touch of self-satisfaction and a sly, shy smile, he said, "So you've noticed my bag. It's clever isn't it? Just a matter of knowing the right fibres to knot together. Of course you have to soak them for a while to make them pliable, but I daresay any fool could have thought of that."

"I never did," I said. "I wish I had; it would be very useful." This, judging from the subtle widening of his smile, was exactly the right response. Unfortunately I added, "Perhaps Adam would have thought of it eventually." At that the smile faded, the serpent marched off ahead of me, not looking back to see if I was following.

A moment later, however, he relented, stopping to ask if I would like one of his oranges. "All warm from the tree," he urged, when I hesitated, "I always carry some with me, they're my favourite fruit." Without waiting for me to accept his offer, he sat down under a clump of tall grasses and took not only an orange from his bag, but also the strange object I had seen him

46

wield on the trees. This time he used it to cut the fruit in half, lengthways, cutting in half again the portion he gave me, so that I could suck the sweetness from the orange quarters, their juices running down my chin. He, on the other hand, slit from top to bottom the skin of his portion, lifted it right off, then ate the fruit neatly, segment by segment.

Afterwards he wiped his fingers on the grass and, taking up his cutting tool, found more trees to tend, lopping small branches here or there, picking off damaged fruit, tearing away creepers which threatened to smother them. Where necessary he shinned up the trees and carried on his labours in their upper branches, while I stood admiring the way his form slid and wound itself so sinuously about trunk and branch, he could almost have been part of whatever tree it was. No matter how firmly, even ruthlessly he pruned, he was never destructive. His loving and delicate care reminded me of his treatment of the insect at our first meeting. Now, as then, I liked him all the better for it, and responded quite willingly when he started encouraging me to help, holding back branches, for instance, or unwinding creepers.

"Did you think the garden flourished by itself?" he asked, as we sat down at last to rest, under a vine hung with pretty bunches not yet ripe enough to eat. "How did you suppose then it had not become entirely overgrown?" Having taken the garden for granted and given the matter no thought at all, I did not answer, merely blushed a little. My eyes, turned away in embarrassment, fell on the cutting tool which lay beside him on the grass. I still distrusted it, as I had done from the beginning, despite the uses to which I had seen it put. At the same time it fascinated, even awed me. The thing he held it by, the handle, was no problem since it was made of wood—though shaped and polished I recognised the curve of the grain. The steel blade was quite another matter. Only the skin of certain fruits, plums for instance, or some varieties of apple, was so smooth and silky. Yet this substance was also hard as stone and still colder to my touch, except when I kept my fingers on it for a while, at which it warmed very quickly.

All the time I examined the thing, the serpent did not take his eyes off me; nor did he move, until, growing bolder, I began to pick it up, whereupon he started, half put out his hand and then withdrew it. Cautiously, meanwhile, I was fitting its handle to my hand—I don't know which fell into place more sweetly and easily, palm to handle, or handle to palm. Even more cautiously I ran the fingers of my other hand along the blade. It was so sharp that despite my care the knife slid into my flesh, minute beads of blood springing up in its path, at which I could only gape having not seen such a thing before. (If a faint memory of Adam's wound, the one from which I had sprung, came to me fleetingly, it did not mean much, though for a moment it made me ache with love and longing.) The cut did not hurt. I was too innocent to be afraid; not so the serpent, who snatched the knife from me and, losing his reluctance to touch my flesh, scrubbed frantically at the blood with a vine-leaf.

He need not have bothered. In a moment there was no blood, the wound, just like Adam's wound, closed itself up as if it had never been, much as a footprint vanishes from wet sand, taking with it the fleeting, inexplicable memory of the rent in Adam's flesh. The serpent, snatching up the knife, stuffed it into his bag, and began gabbling, "God's wonders being performed, no matter how mysteriously, are you not utterly impressed?"

I suspected he was being ironic. I also knew he was very disturbed. He did not wait for me to get up, jumped to his feet and set off at such a furious pace I had to run to catch up with him. In a short while he turned off into a grove of poplar trees and vanished from my sight.

Uneasy, not so much at what had happened as at his response to it, I looked for him for a while, but I found no trace of his golden skin, his lithe and subtle form, and in the end, disconsolate, gave up trying to find him. He'd again left me, to my annoyance, just like the first time we had met, with the sense I had somehow mistreated him; in that way he made me take upon myself his constant fear of betrayal.

Later that day—and I did not look for it, it was an omen of how little, soon, my time was to be my own—I met Lilith sitting under a palm tree; an event as unexpected as our first meeting, otherwise entirely different. There was no jungle here. I'd been walking across a landscape empty of life, apart from insects in the grass and a bird or two so high and far away they barely counted. The air smelt of hay and herbs, I remember, and there were distant hills, only the odd olive grove or group of pines relieving the dry monotony of the country leading up to them. I saw nothing distinctive anywhere except Lilith herself; and except the tree under which she sat. Its trunk was set with scales that reminded me of the serpent's skin, but magnified a hundred times, and it soared up and up into the air, breaking out at last into a shock of brittle fronds, in which an otherwise unnoticeable wind spoke unceasingly, with a hiss and rustle and clack.

I remember that sound more than anything we said. I don't think we did say much that time, despite Lilith making it clear she knew where I'd been earlier, and implying some mockery of the serpent. Much less vivid than on the previous occasion, she appeared subdued and even tired. Though she touched my cheek affectionately when I sat down beside her, she did not look at me, simply returned to examining her feet, her indifferent smile directed at her toes.

But I do not think she was indifferent, any more than I was. We sat companionably for a long time, an hour maybe, or even two, Lilith sneezing occasionally, but much less frequently and violently than the last time we had met. Later, when we parted, I found myself remembering painfully how much smaller her feet were than mine and how much rougher and redder and dirtier. She must have walked, I thought, a great deal further than I had.

Chapter Seven

Twice in the garden Adam danced. The second time was not long before we left Eden, after I'd smelled and longed for the fruit of the tree of life. But the first time I was innocent still, and it makes one of my favourite memories of my husband in the garden.

I'd reached him later than usual, I remember, for I'd been talking to the serpent. Adam did not see me come. He'd already made a shelter for us, on the edge of a beechwood. And meanwhile, on the short grass of the hillside, in the light of the setting sun, he'd begun dancing, music-less, alone.

But he did not need either music or a partner. The one he carried in his head, to judge from the rhythm of his movements, as for the other—he was himself his own partner, anyone else would have been superfluous. It alarmed me for a moment because it was I who was superfluous, obviously; but only for a moment. After that I was too delighted by what I saw to care about any such thing.

It was not that he appeared graceful in the least. If anything he was even more ungainly than usual—I could not help remembering the effortless way in which the serpent moved. Yet there was something very powerful, almost elemental in his clumsiness; in the way he hunched his shoulders and hung his hands a little way in front of him; in the way no part of his labouring body made common cause with any other, yet all of him kept to his unheard beat. I noticed how burly he was, how broad. I also noticed—and it touched me very much—how erratically the sun seemed to have burned him. The top of his shoulders, for instance, had turned dark mahogany, so had his nose which jutted from his face like the beak of some bird. The rest of his body was much paler than that; his belly, where you could see it for hair, was almost white in places. (The serpent on the other hand was burnished all over; every time he moved, a slippery gleam slid the length of his skin.)

Adam was beginning to breathe in heavy gasps now, circling dizzily, his arms spread wide, rivulets of sweat trickling among the forests of hair on his chest. His beard, moreover, reached his chest these days, his hair touched his shoulders, as if the growth of his foliage, unlike that of the trees and bushes, went unpruned. His face tense with concentration, he kept swaying towards where I stood hidden behind a tree and then swaying away again. The sun was all but gone now, only the faintest gleams caught answering gleams from his skin; sometimes he almost vanished in the deepening shadows from the trees.

It was at one such time that I noticed the flickers dancing with him, keeping time with him, less visible when he moved back on to the open hill, burning brighter each time he lurched towards the darkness. Fireflies they must have been; I'd never seen them before. They wove themselves between Adam's arms and legs, brushed his cheeks, spun about his torso like sparks from an invisible fire, making him appear at once more ludicrous and more miraculous. There had been a wind earlier, but it had died now. The only sounds to be heard as I watched him with an ever-increasing confusion of irritation and bewilderment, amazement and awe were Adam's grunts and sighs, the thud, thud, thudding of his feet upon the ground.

In the end he just stopped; fell into the shelter he'd made, and slept. There was a store of apples laid beside it; I ate one gratefully and slid in beside him. He did not appear to wake—all the same he rolled over, clasped me in his arms and made love to me in his sleep. It was a warm night and by the time he'd finished, tired, satisfied and happy, I was running with his sweat as well as with my own.

And so it seems I've come to Adam at last. I am conscious of how little and how faintly I have drawn him up till now. But then it is especially hard for me to describe my husband. It is like severing one of my limbs and examining it from arms' length. And though in Eden, unlike me, he changed very little, after Eden he changed so much—if still not as much as I did—that what he became has quite obscured from me what he was then.

The first fact about Adam, of course, is that he was—is—a maker. Not a maker in the serpent's sense of course; Adam was not an inventor, let alone a smith or builder; such matters of manufacture—the ones with which the serpent dazzled me— terrified my husband. In other words, working wholly inside his head, his task was not to tame and make use of nature, but rather to create it. Oh yes, of course, it was Jehovah who created the world just as afterwards he created us. Yet his earth remained featureless. It was Adam who gave it its contours and covering; who raised the mountains and lowered the valleys, dug the oceans, levelled out the plains. Afterwards he clothed them with trees and plants and grasses, making fields, forests and gardens, all the beauties of the earth.

I don't know when I first became aware that this was Adam's vocation; what he worked at when he left me alone all day. Nor did he ever tell me what he did directly. Yet somehow, through things he let drop, through Jehovah's hints, through the passing gibes of the other inhabitants of Eden, the knowledge filtered through, till I understood it well enough to shout the fact out loud, and did so at last on the day I begged to be allowed to watch him at his work. But he would not let me—I'd distract him, he said, rejecting out of hand my pleas that unless I saw it happening I'd never understand precisely what was meant by the statement that Adam made landscapes; let alone understand—or even be- lieve—this strangest of strange notions that no landscape existed till he had imagined and created it.

(No one of course entirely understood this latter statement. In Eden I lost count of the arguments I was to hear upon the subject. Jehovah claimed, naturally, that it was he who put the ideas which inspired his creation into Adam's head. In some of his discussions with the serpent, the fallen angel Sammael stated, passionately, that this was the only fact that mattered. Yet, as the serpent would immediately point out, Adam's head had not only to be able to contain so many ideas, it also had to express them in a hundred different ways. After all Adam did not just feel hungry and ask for an apple; he asked for many varieties of apple—among them, presumably, the apples on the tree of life. Also, how did he conceive of a pomegranate? Or a coconut? Still more, what unthinkable needs led him to ask for a mountain? A salt lake? A jungle? Where did the partnership between God and Adam begin and where did it end?)

What I did understand, however—as Lilith must have done before me—was the effect this work had on Adam. It was not long before I recognised that on those days he looked abstracted and gazed at me blankly, he was probably seeing one of his own landscapes instead of seeing me. And that on those days he appeared to despair, though everything seemed as usual, it was because he could not see any landscape at all—indeed that on any day he was ecstatic or exhausted, or demanding, or even wonderfully tranquil, it had something to do with the success or failure of his work.

Certainly it did not mean any alteration in his love for me. No matter how wayward his moods, there was no doubt in the beginning how much he loved me. In Eden, often, I fed him fruit from my own hands; plums maybe, or peaches, the kinds having such juicy flesh he'd sup them up greedily and slowly and with unutterable delight, closing his eyes so that he could dwell still more fully on the taste. His tongue would linger on the grooves of the kernel, and then passing it, reach my fingers; his lips would follow; his teeth; he would bite my fingers gently till it seemed he was going to eat me too, was going to swallow me willingly, every bit. You'd have thought he loved me so much he wanted to take me back inside his body.

At the same time, I admit, I noticed a curious bemusement sometimes in the way he looked at me—even in the way he loved me—it was as if he did not quite know why he felt like this or what was happening to him; as if he found each new feeling and encounter still stranger than the last. Indeed the whole experience of love seemed even newer to him than to me. I found this surprising, seeing how much longer he had lived in the garden. I'd have found it a great deal more surprising had I known—as I was painfully to learn—that Adam had already been married.

Chapter Eight

I was happier than ever these days in the garden with Adam—and with Lilith, for I saw her often, though never for very long as yet. Sometimes I only glimpsed her in the distance; sometimes I did not even see her, but simply heard her sneeze. To know she was there, however, delighted if puzzled me, and it did not occur to me to want any more.

I was too busy for one thing. Most days I spent hours in the serpent's company, just him and me at that time. Except for an occasional, faintly mocking shadow on the edge of things, Sammael had not deigned to reveal any more of his presence to me than he had on my wedding night. Nor did the serpent joke or tease or flirt with me; only very occasionally did he allow me to tease him. Even when I failed to appreciate his efforts, he barely allowed himself to take offence, pushing aside all attempts at more frivolous intercourse between us.

Instead he instructed me—how to cultivate the garden, for instance; not just how to tend the plants and trees that were already there, but how to propagate and plant food plants in particular—fruit—vegetables—even crops of wheat. (Though not yet knowing any other use for them, I loved to husk and chew the little nutty grains.)

One day he began to teach me to chip flints to make sharp implements. I asked him why he wouldn't show me how to make a knife like his, but he told me it would involve more dangerous arts than I was yet ready for, or maybe ever would be ready for. For a start I would have to learn to make fire. This was the first time I heard that word, and I did not know what it meant, but he would not tell me the meaning, no matter how much I questioned him.

I was always asking questions these days, like a child made aware suddenly that absolutely nothing should be taken for granted. The serpent encouraged me; indeed he accused me of inattention and blindness if I did not ask questions. In his view if you did not enquire, it meant you had not observed. He himself enquired into everything, as I was to discover in the course of his discussions with Sammael. Adam on the other hand never asked questions, at least not in my hearing. But when I began to ask them he noticed it at once.

Yet I was much too occupied to be more than marginally aware of Adam's increasing suspicion. Perhaps, seeing his displeasure, I was a little less open with him than I had been as to how I spent my days. Yet I had no wish or intention to deceive him. And still, often, the serpent and I grew so absorbed I would allow myself to forget how late it was getting, not setting off to find Adam until it was almost dark, ignoring thereafter his irritable comments.

Ironically enough the day his anger exploded at last was one of the few on which I had not seen any sign of the serpent. I had been a little upset at first when he failed to appear, but after all spent a pleasant enough day, talking to Lilith for a while, then wandering alone, realising that I'd been missing the pleasure of my own company. Later, however, on my way to find Adam, I fell in with some of my friends, the animals; among them that strange creature, the wolf, the only one in the garden whose eyes looked longingly beyond boundaries I was not yet aware of, and who for that reason probably intrigued me, though I did not then see why.

It was late, almost sunset, before I approached the bower that Adam had made in a particularly enchanting spot. Ripe apricots grew overhead, wild strawberries underfoot; far in the distance stood a range of snow-capped mountains.

"Where have you been?" he asked, ignoring my exclamations of delight. His arms hanging at his sides, he waited by the nearest tree, his head poking a little forward as he began to interrogate me, in a tone as agitated as it was uncertain.

"Only talking to the wolf," I said. "Adam, what is wrong with him? Why is he so restless? We're all so happy in the garden, yet with him I've always the feeling he wants to be somewhere else."

"What the wolf wants has nothing to do with us," he replied. "Eve, why must you always question Jehovah's purposes?"

"Why not," I replied lightly, still too happy to notice the danger. "Have some apricots, Adam, they look delicious."

In reply, to my astonishment, he threw the fruit at me. I stood quite still, staring at him, apricots raining about my body. When he had finished I stooped and ate one, almost mechanically, as if I could think of nothing else to do while he was raging and ranting. I had never heard him say so much; about how I never took any notice of him these days, and could not possibly love him as I ought to, as his wife. About how I spent my days gossiping idly with the animals, in particular with that suspicious character the serpent; hadn't the angels warned me about him? They, not I, had told Adam how much time we spent together and about the dangerous, if not blasphemous things he taught me—obviously I'd been deceiving my husband for some reason of my own. On top of that, why was I always asking questions, impugning our creator—our only function was to praise not to question, didn't I realise?

"You speak just like the angels," I replied, shaken and disconsolate. For yes, I admit it, Adam was as pompous as this sounds; but also so unhappy that I pitied him in the same instant that, helplessly, guiltily, I wanted to laugh at him. When he added, more loudly than ever, that if I wasn't careful I'd go the same way as . . . I was too indignant to notice how abruptly his voice halted or even to wonder what it was he had not said. I'd already started to interrupt him, angrily.

"Then what am I supposed to do the whole day long? You always vanish, you never let me come with you, though I've often asked." And then I did laugh, at the expression on his face.

"This is a serious discussion, and all you can do is laugh." He groaned.

A little contrite, I went to put my arms about him. But he shook me off and strode off through the apricot grove, crushing the strawberries beneath his feet while I stumbled after him. Failing to see a branch lying in his path, he tripped and did not fall only because I came close enough to catch him.

Some demon had taken me now, I started laughing again and could not stop. "And when I do walk the garden with you, you only complain I'm getting in your way," I cried, choking with hilarity.

Adam turned and faced me again. "Have you finished?" he asked, his icy voice belying his heated, dishevelled appearance.

"I think so," I said. "But I could go on a great deal longer."

"Shall I tell you what I wish?" He was gazing at me so blankly and impersonally that suddenly I found I was not laughing any more, but stared at him in my turn, appalled.

"Shall I tell you? I wish God had not made you. I wish I was still alone in Eden."

I could not believe what I was hearing; I stared and stared, my eyes seeming to burn in the heat of his. When I turned away at last, I heard him give a huge cry of anguish, then all at once his arms were about me, he was smothering me with kisses, weeping as he did so, and asking me to forgive him. How could he say such dreadful things, of course he wanted me to be there with him in the garden. He loved me, oh how he loved me. I, too, was weeping by now, I believed his words of love as utterly as I believed my own. Given so much proof of his feeling how I could imagine, at that time, that he would ever have regretted my making? Very easily then, I forgave him, telling him that I too did not know what had come over me.

Much later, long after we had retired to bed, I awoke to find Adam snoring heavily at my side, and Jehovah, alternately calling me "Eve" and "Adam's rib" whispering mischievous words that I could not quite hear, though I wanted to. Perhaps he did not intend me to hear, precisely. Half-heard they were like tickling— once I giggled aloud and caught him, definitely, conspiratorially, laughing back at me. This I did not like at all. I clutched Adam's arm, not caring if he woke, and begged hard for Jehovah to go away, wondering why as I did so he never seemed to tease Adam as he teased me, let alone mock him as he mocked the angels; was it because Adam's faith in him was so easy and direct? In which case why did not Jehovah let me worship him as simply as that? It was not that I did not want to; I had never been allowed to. At that thought sleep overtook me once again.

The next morning Adam and I looked at each other warily and did not refer to what had happened. Adam, however, lingered where he would normally have hurried about his business, and kissed me goodbye very sweetly. Afterwards, having gone a little way, he came back to kiss me again.

Contritely, because there had been some justice in his accusations of neglect, and also, less kindly, because I meant it to be a test, I suggested that today I should accompany him at his work.

Adam looked horrified. "Must you take everything I say literally?" he protested.

I smiled and said nothing, and after a little thought Adam gave in; I think, quite genuinely, he did not want to leave me that morning. At this I began to regret my request, but it was he now who was implacable. The angel Raphael appeared while we were arguing the point. He had taken to visiting us early in the day, often bringing some delicacy with him—today it was waxy kernels, nut-like in taste but much softer in texture; pine nuts he called them.

I thought they were delicious and ate very many, but Adam declined them so offhandedly—he still affected to despise the angels—that I grew indignant on Raphael's behalf and in a mischievous moment suggested that he, too, came along. He accepted with alacrity and a slightly shifty glance at Adam, who had been opening his mouth to protest, but shut it again when he saw Raphael looking at him, instead turned a glare on me. Then he marched off, throwing over his shoulder, "Well then, come if you must." He set such a pace I could scarcely keep up with him; Raphael could be heard to pant behind, and looked more like one guarded than guarding.

I do not know what I expected of the day. It was a beautiful one, the high white clouds malleable enough to have taken any shape. But they remained mere clouds, just as the country we walked in remained entirely familiar, and we could discover only places that Adam had already made. He grew more and more baffled and frustrated. After a while, it was obvious he blamed me and Raphael for his problems, glaring at us alternately, not that Raphael cared.

"No doubt inspiration does come much less easily on some days than others," he exclaimed helpfully, at last. The glower Adam offered in response did not seem to daunt him. "Of course art can never be easy," he went on, adding, good-humouredly, when Adam made no reply, "Tell me, Adam, what gives you your ideas?"

Even then I could not quite believe he was in earnest. But when I looked at him, his expression revealed nothing but interest and concern. He seemed, moreover, to be struggling to develop his thoughts; in another moment, he appeared to have succeeded. "The source of your inspiration must be God of course. But in what way does he manifest the forms to you? Would that, perhaps, be a more accurate way of putting it, Adam?" he asked. His head slightly on one side, he wore an expression in which sympathy and interest combined.

Adam quickened his step, clearly attempting to outpace both of us, but Raphael, continuing to propose interesting questions, kept up with him easily though I soon dropped behind. In a while they were both out of sight. I could not even hear the sound of Raphael's voice.

The country was changing now. There was less and less herbiage, only tumbled rocks and boulders and hilly outcrops, rising progressively to some higher hills. I saw lichen in the crevices and sometimes, close to the sand, a few pinkish plants with fleshy leaves and stems. Once I came on a scatter of small melons, their surfaces mottled like snake or lizard skins. I gathered one and broke it open to find it full of seeds but fleshless, while its juice when I applied my tongue was bitter. Not part of God's bounty, I thought, recalling the phrase Raphael invariably used when he brought us some offering.

It was indeed a desert that I saw—there were deserts in Eden, if you chose to look for them. The difference from the deserts outside Eden was this: they did not teach me anything about hunger and thirst. Their sun, blazing in an empty sky, might suggest pain, but was not yet permitted to inflict it, nor were the stones I trod on nor the thorns that pricked me anything more than sensations; some, admittedly, not altogether pleasant. As for their distances, much as I liked them, they weren't mine to reach by my own painful struggle. I was just a visitor, not an inhabitant, innocently marvelling at all the different shapes and colours I noticed in the tumbled rocks.

Perhaps Adam one day would clothe their nakedness. Perhaps he had done, once upon a time—when I looked closely I saw forms locked deep inside the stone; insects and fishes, huge, clawed footprints; I even saw leaves and flowers, delicately delineated in a substance that otherwise seemed to have nothing to do with them.

I hurried after Adam now bursting with questions—he would have needed a new language to answer most of them; a language he of all creatures lacked. Though I knew that perfectly well, I chose to find his continued silence perverse. My temper rising with the heat I exploded in a way which surprised even me, screaming at him that I wanted to know these things, why wouldn't he tell me?

Raphael calmed me in the end, for his own purposes, no doubt. He told me how thoughtful and observant I was, and said he was sure God must be pleased I observed his creation so closely, but that only he, of course, knew the answers to such matters.

"Then why does he provide no answers?" I asked, weary suddenly, my voice containing only the last few drops of an anger no less astonishing to me now than to others. I sat myself down on a smooth black rock, and as I did so saw that Adam had gone some way away and was sitting on the sand with his back to us.

He sat there hours, it seemed. The sun ate its way into my bones, meanwhile, and out the other side. Until at last, suddenly, Adam gave a great cry. "Volcano," he shouted; nothing more. But at that the sun grew so bright it ate up the whole landscape. I could see nothing but brightness, into which exploded suddenly a conical mountain; from which exploded what? *Fire?* But it was the first time I had seen fire, so I could not name it, let alone connect its appalling glory with what the serpent had refused to show me. It belched not only flames; it belched rocks and soot and a cloud of smoke and then more flames, as if it had swallowed the sun and, unable to digest it, spat it out again. Besides this it was vomiting out the liquid rock I saw flowing down its conical sides towards me. But we were too far for the mineral river to reach. The boulder on which I sat had petrified long ago.

I ran to Adam, again full of questions—but they died on my lips as I saw how white and tired he looked. "Thank you, Eve, for inspiring me," was all he could say. Which did not satisfy me at all, but I saw it would have to do for the moment, and withdrew to let Adam gather himself together. Raphael, however, was less kind. We had hardly begun to wend our way back to more fruitful places when Uriel and Gabriel and Michael joined us, and I have no doubt it was Raphael who summoned them. Instantly, and in unison, they broke into a song of praise to his latest creation so soaring and passionless it was at the same time profound mockery of Adam's work. Adam did not notice of course. Everyone mocked him in Eden—except for Jehovah— yet he never noticed. I do not think he had vanity enough.

Chapter Nine

My next meeting with Lilith, as unexpected as such meetings always were, coincided with my encountering for the second time the trees of life and death and the river that encircled them.

Though I had by no means forgotten the trees that Jehovah had shown us—indeed my curiosity about them had been growing by the day—I had not been looking for them that morning. Nor had I been looking for Lilith. I found the river first and did not recognise it till it was more or less at my feet. There were rushes, with plumed crests, and poplars, having smooth white trunks. Overhanging the water were willow trees, yellow-flowered creepers wreathed round them, their roots exposed where the currents had eaten away the river bank. Some of the trees and their nets of creeper were suspended so giddily above the water that I wondered how they stayed upright. At that very moment a tree came floating past, fallen recently enough for its leaves to be still green. I even saw a nest in its branches and a bird sitting on it patiently, while its earth-covered roots reached out towards me imploringly like hands.

"A pretty sight don't you think?" said Lilith's voice behind me, adding immediately, "I'm sorry, if I startled you." For I had jumped in alarm at the sound of her voice and her unexpected touch upon my arm.

"You always do," I said, in confusion, remembering the many ways in which she had managed to startle me.

But she did not try to startle or confuse me now. Indeed she appeared very tender, laying soft hands upon my shoulders and kissing me gently upon the lips.

"Well, how is it with you, Eve?" she inquired in a kindly voice, as if she genuinely wanted to know.

"Very well," I answered, half-softened already by her kindness, and in a moment let her take my hand and lead me to sit under a poplar tree, her arm flung lightly about my shoulders.

"Tell me everything you've been doing," she insisted, brushing aside all my inquiries as to her own activities. I was quite unguarded now; her apparently avid interest in everything I had to tell her led me to describe at last my argument with Adam in the apricot grove, so releasing her sharp tongue. ("Oh really Eve, what a good little wife you are; why are you so placatory always, don't you feel degraded by it?")

She modified her tone when I fell silent, drew me closer to her, and said much more gently, "Poor Eve, how I torment you."

"It's not that. My thoughts aren't quick enough, I don't know how to answer," I replied.

"I do not always know how to answer myself," was her response. I did not believe her. Maybe she did not want me to believe her. Either way we sat in silence for a while, the sun falling through the poplar branches, dappling our flesh in its light and shade. Unfamiliar birds warbled delightfully overhead. One bird with a yellow underside and a long tail paraded in front of us, its tail dipping and flickering. Another hopped from Lilith's shoulder on to mine in a very familiar way. At the same time two small iridescent lizards began to run about our thighs, freezing briefly from time to time and regarding us, their heads on one side, their paws spread out, before flicking into life again; flick, freeze, they went; flick, freeze.

I could have stayed watching them the whole morning, if not the whole day. But Lilith suddenly leapt to her feet, ran to the edge of the river, and after one glance back at me, dived in, head-first.

Without a moment's thought I followed her, cast myself head-long also, arms outstretched, and hit the water flat knocking all the breath out of me though I felt no pain. Thereafter, the river far deeper than last time I had crossed it, I went on sinking, descending through the water with a series of sensations so new and strange and on which I reflected so earnestly it never occurred to me that I ought rather to be thinking how to extricate myself.

I saw weed in the water, also fishes, snails and beetles, also the silver bubbles and flickers of the water's movement. I felt my mouth fill up with it—what overwhelmed me chiefly, I suppose, at that moment, was the fear of death, only I did not recognise it for what it was; how could I? This was Eden. By now, moreover, against all evidence, I was sure my lungs could use water as easily as they used air; it explained, no doubt, the calm way in which, like a dying man, I observed the events of my life from my birth—perhaps even from before my birth—chasing through my head. Maybe I could have surrendered entirely to that jumble of memories and sensations; could have let the rush of water against my skin, the slide of fishes across my open eyes, the pull of the weeds, the interminable contrary visions, turn the breathless shock of the river into a cool and comfortable entombment. Instead, suddenly, I let the water push me upwards, and broke into light and air, coughing and spluttering.

I do not know whom I expected to see then—not Lilith perhaps—but it was Lilith that I saw. She was laughing at my splutters and kicking out with her arms and legs. I might have sunk again, had I not been able, somehow, to respond—the next moment I too had begun paddling with my hands and feet and was even contriving to stay afloat. It did not occur to me to be afraid of failing; if she could do it then so could I. Before long I had managed to struggle to the far side of the river and up its muddy bank where I collapsed at the foot of the tree of death, too exhausted to be aware of Lilith sneezing out the river above my head, let alone to recognise the tree or its companion, blossomless by now.

Lilith seemed to have no respect for either tree. In a moment I even saw her reach nonchalantly up and snatch one of the fig tree's large leaves, on which she proceeded to dry herself energetically, staring at me throughout, her look between amusement and enquiry. She did not speak. Nor, shaking myself, the way an animal does to get rid of the water, did I. I was gathering my hair up and starting to wring it out when I saw her open her legs without a hint of self-consciousness and start to dry between them.

The same secrets lay there as lay between my legs, I observed. I gazed with awe and fascination while her vigorous scrubbing separated the hairy divisions and revealed for a moment their more tender, moist and very pink interiors. In that moment, dazed as I still was, I found myself overcome by a profound sense of loss that I could not understand at all, having no clear memory of Adam's wound. Yet I knew I had known another such wounded place, and that it was precious to me. In a blaze of love I stretched up and placed my lips against that wound of hers. It was only for a moment; I astounded myself; yet Lilith did not seem surprised.

"What of it?" she asked when I apologised. There were still drops of water clinging to her body. The way she had tied back her wet hair, I would barely have recognised her, her face so fully revealed appearing both more ancient and more childlike than I had seen it before. Though her eyes and her smile were the same, she looked altogether less exotic, if no safer to know, like a wicked imp instead of an intractable female angel.

"You know of course what trees these are?" she asked me.

"Of course," I replied impatiently, having no interest in the trees at that moment.

"And you know, of course, not to eat their fruit?"

"Who would want to?" I replied, pulling down a branch to inspect one of the little green nodules. It had swelled, I noticed, since I saw it last. And on the apple tree already were the tiniest of green apples.

"Jehovah did tell us we might eat these," I said, adding hastily, "but they're not ready yet. And in any case, when they are Adam and I intend to eat them together."

We had never in fact discussed the matter, Adam and I. In fact, since our wedding day, we had not mentioned either fruit. I lied, without having known I was going to, because I felt wary suddenly and even embarrassed for reasons I did not understand; the expression on Lilith's face was bland enough, and her fingers explored another fig leaf as if nothing else was of interest.

"Why not come with me to find Adam?" I went on; which was one more possibility I'd never considered seriously till the second that I spoke. Immediately I was filled with such pleasure at the prospect of being in the company of both my husband and my friend I could not think why not.

"And whatever made you ask that?" inquired Lilith, giving an ambiguous smile.

"Why not?" I replied. "Why not?" And to her repeated "Why?" said, bewilderedly, "Because I love you both." And yet as I spoke there came again the sudden uneasiness, sudden as the delectable smell which floated all at once from the unripe apples and then disappeared again. I must have imagined it, I thought, and added, a little desperately, "We could sit and eat together, don't you think? Adam and I always eat fruit together in the evenings."

"What a pleasant and domestic picture you present." Lilith's voice was not especially unkind; she spoke reflectively and appeared to be thinking, resting her head against the trunk of the fig tree. A small breeze crept up from the river. The pale light on her face still so much more naked than usual revealed dark spaces beneath her eyes and faint blemishes on her skin which moved me, though I did not recognise them for what they were, any more than I was to recognise the first signs of ageing I saw on Adam in the desert. I only knew that I felt for her at that moment a melancholy tenderness that made me want to take her in my arms and embrace her.

But I did not dare, not then, while she looked at me as if she pitied me, and asked, "Well, am I pretty enough for Adam? What kind of fruit does he like best? And is he talkative, or does he just sit and grunt and pick his teeth?" At that she burst out laughing and turned away; in a moment had loosed her hair and shaken it out, and looked precisely as I had always known her, brilliant, exotic, puzzling, and seductively dangerous.

"I'm hungry," she said. "Will you let me share your meal?"

But it was I who doubted now; I stammered and prevaricated, and she, fully aware of my doubts, went on, teasingly, "Don't you want me after all? What a shame. I had such a pretty scene in my head, how we'd sit under a wild cherry tree together and Adam would hand me peaches and apricots while you protested he hadn't given me the sweetest; and then both of you would search for the most perfect and unblemished fruit, simply to give to me. How loved I'd feel then. I daresay even Jehovah would heap blessings on my head."

She had never referred to Jehovah before by name. I looked at her alarmed, because I did not know whether to take her seriously.

"Don't just sit there with your mouth open, Eve," Lilith said sharply. She was not joking now. Irritable suddenly, she brushed away my hand as if it were one of the lizards that had run about our bodies earlier, and set off at a brisk pace towards the river.

Upset and angry I cried after her, "Lilith, where are you going, come back?" but she only turned and hissed at me, "Why should I, what is there to come back for?"

"I'm sure Adam will love you as I do," I heard myself protesting; at which she stopped dead, and cried venomously, "How dare you, Eve. What a presumptuous thing to say. Perhaps you didn't realise; in which case you can add stupidity to all your other faults."

I stared at her aghast—held back my tears from simple pride, but in doing so I hated my friend. I even clenched my fists, raised one as if to hit her—I felt I could actually have punched her, wanted to the more not less when she, seeing it, proceeded to shrivel before my very eyes as if that single burst of anger had contained such force it had sucked her dry. For a moment she regarded me with a blank and weary look. Then she shook herself impatiently, and, a light returning to her eyes, inquired politely, in a slight show of interest, "Were you truly about to hit me, Eve? Did I goad you so very badly?"

It was my turn to shrug now. Dumbly I lowered my fists, more confused than angry, angry only because she was confusing me again.

"Maybe not," I mumbled.

"What a pity," she said indifferently; adding a moment later, "But I am very hungry, Eve, and very tired. I think I will leave you now. You can introduce me to Adam another time, if you still want to. Goodnight, sweetheart. We shall meet again quite soon."

She touched my lips with her hand, and was gone, before I'd had time to say another word, leaving me to struggle back across the river alone. Then I walked home to Adam thoughtfully, still dripping wet, after a day in which without being aware of it I'd come closer than before to both birth and death, though neither of the two meant anything to me yet.

Chapter Ten

I have told already of my final meeting with Sammael. I cannot, however, tell of the first, because it could not be said that we did meet, in the normal sense of the word. Encounter might be a better way of putting it; even then it was a matter of my encountering him, not the other way about—and by processes which made me aware of his existence long before I saw him directly.

I have described the shadow hovering at the edges of our wedding day. By degrees this shadow evolved into a presence, like and not like the presence of the more familiar angels who had, unlike Sammael, declined to rebel. Then one evening the presence took shape, for when I came upon the serpent, there was Sammael also, both of them hunched over a curious chequered board set with carved figures. I could not make any sense of this strange game, played in total silence. When I dared to inquire, the serpent would not answer my questions as he usually did, merely waved me quiet with an impatient hand.

I saw Sammael frequently thereafter, yet always in the serpent's company, as if the serpent alone had the power to conjure him. Sometimes they would be playing the same incomprehensible game—a kind of chess—I don't know which of them had invented it. The parts of kings, queens, bishops and knights were taken by the different ranks of angel, the castles were trees, the pawns all human figures. Why so many I came to wonder, since mankind at that time consisted of Adam, and Lilith, and myself? I would watch, apprehensively, while they were swept off the board one by one, either to Sammael's advantage or the serpent's, until seraphim or cherubim, princedom or power confronted each other alone, and the game appeared to be over. How it was lost or won I never wholly understood; sometimes only the demeanour of the players revealed to me the winner. Sammael shrugged his shoulders either way, less ruefully, perhaps, if he had won. The serpent seemed to show his pleasure or displeasure more openly, but that may have been because I knew him better.

As I have said they played their game in silence, usually so profound it overtook the whole area round them. Birds did not venture to sing; no small animals dared rustle the undergrowth. Consequently I'd expect to encounter them long before they came in sight, as I did also on those many occasions they engaged in the intellectual arguments that were their other mode of competition, as noisy as the first was silent. Those times their voices would echo across the garden with scarcely a pause between; where one voice ceased, the other went on—in the heat of their argument they often overlapped. When I appeared on the scene they took no more notice of me than they did when they were playing their game—the serpent might smile barely, but Sammael always declined to acknowledge my presence, though he did sometimes make use of me in his discourse.

Discourse, by the way, is the right word for Sammael's conversation. He did not talk like you or me, he discoursed with wit and fluency, with a sarcastic and mannered eloquence, not simply of his voice and thought, but of his whole body—inasmuch as he had a body; often it seemed as if he did not. The clearest memory I have of him is of white, supple hands displayed against an area of darkness, turning, twisting, outstretched—sometimes they moved unceasingly, at others were held still in an effective, even theatrical attitude. He was vain of his hands, I think; his ostentatious display of them as necessary a part of his argument as his, to me, frequently unfathomable logic.

I am not stupid. The further reaches of his arguments (almost all revolving round the nature of God—What Jehovah *was*—also the nature of his commandments, which Sammael would claim as indefinable and not to be questioned, before going on to define and question them at length) were not usually beyond my thought, just way beyond my patience and interest. Seeing no point in their interminable reworkings of the meaning of this word or that, I preferred almost from the beginning to direct my attention to the sound of Sammael's voice or the expression on the serpent's face; above all to those elegant hands, darting hither and thither, independently, like fishes in a river.

It was for this reason, I suppose, that I can remember few details of what they talked about and only a little of the substance; and that where I did remember it was usually for some irrelevant reason. For instance if more of the first argument I heard remains in my head than most, it wasn't because it was the first, and its subject—whether gender and sexual division were fundamental to God and his creation—directed in part at me; it was because it took place in the very same apricot grove where Adam and I had quarrelled, with its view of icy mountains. Not that either Sammael or the serpent seemed aware of what a delectable spot it was, any more than Adam had been on that occasion. I, however, can no longer taste the sweet roughness of such strawberries against my tongue, without hearing Sammael proclaiming with his usual chilly passion that angels had no gender, were therefore above gender, which meant that God must be above gender too.

This claim, I remember, drew from an irritated serpent a surprisingly crude response. (Sammael's claims often did I was to discover; such lofty detachment from physical reality demanded earthy answers.) "You mean you have no balls, Sammael?" he asked; driving Sammael in his turn to accuse the serpent of dishonouring the name of God—blessed be his name—Sammael's speech, like that of all angels, was full of such pieties. Whereupon the serpent pointed out that no one had dishonoured God's name more than Sammael, in disobeying him.

Naturally Sammael did not accept that. He insisted that his refusal to bow down to Adam had honoured God, in attempting to maintain the purity of his original design which Jehovah himself had distorted when he raised up the man and the woman. (Sammael always referred to us as "the man" and "the woman" and even in doing so, never bothered to glance my way.) It was the first time I heard him making this astonishing assertion, by no

means, however, the last—in everything to do with his passionate love and hate of God, and his equally passionate desire for
revenge, Sammael remained constant to the end.

His constancy misled me I think, a fact I need to consider
briefly before relating how the arguments concluded that day in
the apricot grove. For it revealed so much pain I could not help
pitying him. Indeed I found the passion for revenge in which his
pain resulted altogether more comprehensible, and much less
terrifying than the purer, quite inhuman passion for justice of the
other angels. This was probably the main reason I failed to
recognise with either my feelings or my mind the raw contradic-
tion at the heart of Sammael's reasoning (at the heart of Sammael,
come to that); his confusion between love and hate.

The serpent, however, did not miss it—not surprisingly I
suppose, since he and I (the one to be mutilated on account of
Sammael, his friend, the other made pregnant by the genderless
Sammael) were to experience the split in Sammael's mind more
fully than anyone. Yet on that day and others I was astonished by
the alarm and even fury with which the serpent attacked what he
called Sammael's slippery arguments, protesting that he jumped
from one topic to another ignoring the yawning gaps between,
and using every excuse to make the point that in his opinion
Sammael was always splitting thought from thought, and all
thoughts from action.

Sammael, while not replying to his accusations directly, clearly
did not like them at all. Indeed, in his pursuit of revenge, he
stooped, not for the last time, to making use of me. First he
steered the conversation towards the matter of gender, then he
inquired as to whether in that and other matters men and animals
were the same. When the serpent maintained that they were,
Sammael asked blandly if this meant he considered there was no
fundamental difference between Adam and himself. The serpent
answered, passionately, he was certain there was not.

Something must have been distracting him that day—he
would not have fallen so neatly otherwise into the trap that had
been set him. For Sammael was now able to suggest, triumphantly, that the serpent thought he and Adam were the same because

he wanted to *be* Adam; and for *many* different reasons. Here—it was first and only time—the fallen angel glanced at me, arranging his hands as he did so into an elegant and effective gesture. The serpent's eyes also veered in my direction; I would have avoided if I could his shifty and horrified look, instead succeeded in meeting it squarely. Hastily as I looked away I could not fail to see the way he flinched before my gaze, let alone the extent of his anger and discomfort. His scales seemed to have lost their pleasant sheen, his body its fluency.

Dismayed and frightened by the repulsion I saw in him, I ran away and wept, assuming he did not like me any more. I did not know enough then to realise how near the mark Sammael's taunt had come, let alone how much the serpent feared my observing what he felt about such matters, or how ambivalent he was in his feelings towards me.

He hid in consequence, for several days afterwards, and when we met again, behaved at first with a studied coolness which hurt my feelings very much, and which, for a little while, made the taste of wild strawberries objectionable to me.

I do not know whether there was any connection. But it was certainly from about this time that the serpent began to teach, far more hectically, the skills I would need in my desert future, not that I knew it then. Some of them, moreover, were skills bound sooner or later to bring me into unwilling conflict with Adam.

Chapter Eleven

Before Lilith showed it to me I never knew there was a wall round the garden. I took it for granted at first like everything else in Eden, laying my hand gladly against its warm stone, my curiosity perhaps not fully aroused till I noticed the branches of a tree peering over it from the other side. Its leaves set in clusters of five like the fingers of my open hand, it might have been begging to come in.

Lilith shook her head at my questions. Why had I never noticed the wall before, I asked, why hadn't Adam pointed it out to me? Had he made it, I insisted, as he made all the rest? He'd always given me the impression that the garden went on for ever, and now I could see that it did not.

Lilith even looked wistful at this, I thought. "That's how Adam is," she suggested at long last. And then added more sharply, "Don't you *know* how Adam is?" Tossing back her head she gave a peal of her mocking laughter and cried, "Eve, Eve, if you only knew how irritating it is, when you look hurt like that." Immediately she walked on ahead of me, stab-stabbing at the ground like a petulant bird with particularly short, quick steps, while I followed, disconsolate, casting no more than one last glance at the sunny wall behind us, since I did not yet feel the need to be anywhere different.

Growing still more at home thereafter, enjoying everything in Eden so fervently I might have known that such bliss could not last for ever, I remained able for the moment to climb its hills and roam its plains, without wondering more than idly what lay outside it, on the other side of the wall. Sometimes I was lazy, lounging all day in the shade making garlands and listening to the music of the garden. Sometimes I exercised myself energetically—it was at this time, emboldened by my experience with Lilith, that I began, tentatively at first, to swim in the rivers and lakes of Eden. Soon I played in the water among fish and otters and other water beasts as confidently and freely as I ran on dry land alongside the hare and the horse or swung fearlessly in the treetops among the brilliant birds, the squirrels and the apes, not expecting to fall any more than they expected to, but sure that the air would cushion me if I did.

Many days I wandered alone; on others some animal might keep me company, or the ever attentive and seemingly benevolent Raphael. Most often, however, I would find at my side the cleverest of my friends, the serpent.

My walks with him of course were almost always to some purpose. Having learned some of the arts of cultivation, I now learned to recognise and name not only all the plants he tended, but many others he did not, also to know their uses, practical, nutritional, even medical; from which, for instance, came fibres strong enough for our ropes and bags and hammocks, which were good to eat, which poisonous, which had bitter juice and which sweet, which would make me sleepy or elate me or soothe any minor aches.

Still, though, I had not persuaded him to teach me to make fire and to fashion a knife like his. But one morning, a week or so after the argument with Sammael, having shrugged, indifferently, at all my previous entreaties, the serpent suddenly said, as indifferently, that he supposed there was no harm in demonstrating fire at least, even if he didn't yet consider it time for me to use it. Saying which he produced his knife again and with it a small flint-stone, meanwhile ordering me to find some dry sticks. I obeyed eagerly, too curious to mind the peremptoriness of his tone (though I did not much like the way he flinched away from me when I touched his arm by mistake, saying, "Mind where you're going" very sharply.)

I hardly saw what happened next; with a harsh scraping sound the blade of his cutting tool met in some way the surface of the flint-stone, drawing out of it a flash of harsh light so brief as to be almost imperceptible. While I was still wondering if I'd imagined it, there followed another. It ran, or seemed to run, against one of the twigs he'd ordered me to hold ready, from which suddenly blossomed—it is the only way I can describe it, though much swifter than blossoming—a brilliant orange petal that danced and jumped and took different shapes as it passed itself on to other twigs, multiplying the while till a whole bouquet of flames was leaping at our feet. Exclaiming with pleasure, I put my hand out and touched them—though I could feel the heat in all its fury it did not burn, and seeing me so impressed and pleased, the serpent looked more comfortable than he had done for days, even smiled a little, his scales gleaming pleasantly in the light of the flames. When I said, "It's like the volcano I saw, that Adam made," he replied, "Yes of course, didn't you realise you were seeing fire?"

But he wouldn't tell me anything else, nor, no matter how much I begged him, show me how he'd made it. In a little while, my pile of twigs consumed, he let it burn itself out till only the ashes remained, glowing very faintly, and even these he extinguished with his foot, rather brutally I thought.

Afterwards he taught me to make a shelter; not by such magic as Adam used for his bowers, but by much more practical means, planting wooden staves upright in the ground and lacing twigs and brushwood and creeper around them, setting rushes over the top to make a roof. He worked me so hard that by the end of the day I was proficient enough to return to the place where I was due to meet Adam and make one for us, as a surprise. (Though not before I'd wasted some considerable time scraping flint on flint, to see if I could make fire and surprise him even more.)

My bower wasn't, of course, as pretty as one of Adam's, made out of living trees. Still, since I had used flowering creepers and leafy branches it was not unpleasant to look at, besides being snug and serviceable. I was pleased with myself and taken aback when instead of praising it Adam said, "Why do you bother with such a thing? Doesn't God provide for us well enough?"

Whereupon he put out his hand and in the usual commodious and obliging fashion a cherry tree transformed itself into a second shelter alongside the one on which I had worked so hard.

He had never enraged me more than at that moment. Without thinking I lifted my hand and wordlessly commanded the cherry tree to desist—it did, immediately. There came an instant expression of amazement upon Adam's face, but I doubt if either his astonishment or terror were as great as mine. Tentatively, beneath my voice, I asked the tree to become a bower, again it obeyed me; I ordered it to desist; it desisted; to reform itself again; so it did. I hardly dared stop the progression in case I lost the knack, and at last, the unfortunate cherry tree continuing obediently to bow and raise itself, bow and raise itself, I burst out laughing, it all seemed so absurd.

Adam did not laugh; for a while he looked more bemused than ever. At last, flinging his arms round me he cried out how marvellous it was, that if I had such gifts he and I would be able to work together in future, I would be his true helpmeet. Think what wonders we might work between us, God willing, he said, rather breathless by now.

I'm afraid that I revealed myself immediately in a much less generous light. His words dissolving my amusement, I ordered the tree to take its natural shape, then left it to its own devices while I unpicked Adam's arms and held him at a distance. In a minute, I let go of him altogether, almost pushed him away from me. He looked crestfallen and again rather puzzled—but I could not, would not spare him, heard myself saying as tactfully as I could, which was not very tactful since I hardly knew what I was going to say before I did:

"No, Adam, that kind of magic is not for me, I'd rather manage in my own way. Don't look so surprised. I've things to make, no less than you have. I don't know quite how yet, but I will make them, all the same, as I can, above all as I want to, not as you and Jehovah decide."

I remember thinking, Lilith will approve of this; even as I looked at the unhappy Adam, sadly and guiltily. Meanwhile, experimentally, I again ordered the tree to change its shape, but

78

it, at least, seemed to have taken me at my word, and did not listen any more, remaining tree not bower.

We slept in Adam's bower that night. It was the least I could do, I felt. Adam too subdued to demand it, I had no need to concede the point. I did not dismantle my shelter, however, which remained in all its crudity alongside Adam's cherry tree. Its flowers were dead by morning, unlike the cherry blossom, whose petals fell gently, covering our bed. My hair was full of the white petals. Before he went away Adam brushed them out gently, looking at me uncertainly as he did so. Since last night he had hardly said a word; I would almost have welcomed one of the rages by which he still responded, for instance, to any of my conversations with the animals I was unwary enough to mention. I daresay I could have roused one in him now by pointing out that the serpent had taught me my new skill; but I could not bring myself to do that. We parted without either of us having made one reference to what had happened, though it would have been perverse of me not to have regretted my brief magic a little.

Chapter Twelve

I had not seen Lilith for a day or two, or even thought about her much, except to wonder briefly when she would come to meet Adam, and to feel relieved she had not turned up on the night I made the bower. When she did arrive a few evenings later, it was without further invitation let alone warning. (On my taxing her with this later, she claimed she did not need an invitation, she had already been given one.)

It's true, I think, she would not have turned up unless I'd invited her. But that, like all my attempts at getting my friends together, was my mistake, though it never occurred to me at the time it might be one, not even after I'd seen how violently Adam started on catching sight of her. He had been carrying several peaches, all of which slipped from his grasp and began rolling hither and thither on the ground.

"What a pleasant domestic scene," she said, politely. "I've brought my contribution to supper. Am I allowed to join in?"

So there it was. Yet now I come to it, I do not find myself willing or able to describe that evening in any detail; it is not a particularly cheerful memory, also very confusing, the first of others I'd prefer to forget. It makes me realise, moreover, in my inexorable—and in most ways baffling—advance towards the eating of the fig, that from now on my story will seem more difficult to tell.

Nothing went disastrously wrong; indeed little happened, and nothing whatever was directly revealed. Once the first shock had passed it would be hard to say which of them, Adam or Lilith, kept up more effectively their mutual pretence of never having set eyes on each other. All the same the meeting between my husband and my friend was by no means the joyful occasion I'd imagined, though not for any reason I could easily understand.

Why did the scent of the trees beneath which we sat seem so cloying, I wondered? It had always pleased me before. And why did Adam speak only in blank monosyllables? And why did everything Lilith say have such an uncomfortable edge to it, of mockery, or ill-temper or sometimes both at once? I thought I must be imagining this at first, but as the evening wore on it became clear that I was not. For instance she'd brought mangoes, a fruit I'd never tried before, and when I remarked how strange they tasted she asked, very sharply, "Whatever do you mean, Eve? They taste perfectly good to me."

Haltingly I tried to explain that despite finding the fruit as sweet and fleshy as a peach I found its aftertaste not sweet at all—not sour either, not in the least sour, but—Lilith interrupted me. "You mean they taste very slightly rotten? That is exactly the charm of mangoes. You should try to be more precise."

Adam opened his mouth. For a moment I thought he was going to defend me—but having looked from Lilith to me, and back again at Lilith, he shrugged and desisted, as if he did not want to be involved, emphasising the point by staring up into the tree above our heads and whistling softly a phrase too tuneless to identify; at least I could not identify it, though it made me feel uncomfortable. Or perhaps it was a premonition of betrayal that sent a haze creeping over the garden; not the haze of dusk, something much gloomier. The comfortable distances beyond our pleasant grove seemed to have shrunk in the evening light.

We grew merrier later. Maybe the coconut milk that we drank had fermented a little. Adam in particular appeared more cheerful than he had been all evening. He even laughed sometimes at Lilith's teasing, and once, rather clumsily, he grabbed her hand and forced her to put a peeled grape into his mouth just as a moment ago, unasked, she had put one into mine. By now he was laughing very loudly indeed, almost wildly, and when Lilith stopped to peel more grapes I saw him watching her covertly, as if she fascinated him. Perhaps I realised then for the first time the implications of her being an attractive woman; or just another woman, come to that. The pain I felt was jealousy, presumably—I couldn't name it, having never felt such a thing before, but I did not like it in the least. The next grape Lilith laid upon my lips I almost spat away in a welter of emotions I was unable to understand—maybe it was not the scent of the trees but the scent of Lilith I found so stifling.

Indeed, I could not bear to remain close to them any longer. I turned my back and walking to the edge of the grove, laid my cheek against the rough, spicy bark of a cinnamon tree. It was almost dark by now—when I glanced back towards them, I could barely see either Lilith or my husband. I could hear them, however. It was as if my departure had relieved them in some way, for both sounded easier. Lilith was talking, her tone equable enough. I could not hear precisely what she said, but I could hear the laugh Adam gave in answer. Did I just imagine it or had they actually moved much nearer to each other? Was there something conspiratorial in the way they bent their heads together? As I abandoned my tree and crept back into the centre of the glade, I could have sworn that one of them—was it Lilith?—asked "Did you?" lowering their voice so much I could not hear the rest. To which the other—was it Adam?—returned an emphatic "No."

At that moment Lilith noticed me returning through the gloom. "Here comes your charming wife, Adam," she said very loudly. He started in surprise and swung round to find me standing just behind him. "We were just talking about you, Eve," Lilith continued. "Singing your praises, naturally. I was telling Adam what a lucky man he was to have found you after all this time."

Adam merely glowered at this. I did not think it very gallant or kind of him. But then, my suspicions aroused—who knows in what direction—I did not feel that I trusted Lilith either, trusting her even less when she came towards us, placed Adam's arms about me, stepped back again and crooned, "Oh let me look at you. What a charming sight—a perfect picture of matrimony."

At which Adam removed his arms, pushing me from him so

violently I'd have fallen if Lilith had not caught me between her hands; then he turned his back on us and walked briskly away.

"How many mountains did you make today, Adam?" Lilith shouted after him; a strange question I thought, though it did not occur to me till later to wonder how she knew he made mountains. Did she go to watch him? If so, did he know she did?

Much later when she'd departed and we'd retired to bed, Adam lay apart from me in silence. Doing my best to forget my vague fears and doubts I phrased questions meanwhile that I did not manage to ask as to what he thought of her; until, suddenly, he rolled on top of me and began stroking me with an unusual fervour—a reminiscent fervour, I suspect, though naturally I did not recognise it, and assumed my discomfort came from the over-insistent fragrance of the tree which sheltered us. But when his embraces were done—in all other respects they were satisfactory, serving to reassure me a little after such a disturbing evening. While he lay snoring as usual, I remained awake. At length I found the scent so stifling that I crept out of the bower and walked in the dark till I could smell it no longer.

I wandered a long time that night, listening to owls; their hooting I was certain had something to do with Lilith—indeed I think now they may have been Lilith, or Lilith may have been them. In such a mood the last thing I wanted was a confrontation with Jehovah. Probably that was why he came; alternatively he came because he thought the questions running through my head on this significant evening were intended for him.

It is true, certainly, that I had found myself asking some very difficult questions—not just about the garden but about those with whom I shared it; above all, for the first time, questions about myself. It does not mean that I expected him to answer them. I'd given up expecting Jehovah to answer anything; his response to any query was always to pose another. (Why do you speak to me in riddles? I had demanded of him once, only to be asked what I meant by the word riddle?)

He asked me another question now; how I, Eve, in other words Adam's Rib—I still did not know what he meant by that—had enjoyed my evening between Lilith and my husband. A way of putting it that might have proved some kind of answer had I known where to find it. But that night in my weary innocence, I had no idea where to begin. I could only reply, petulantly I fear, "Very much indeed. Which of course you know, since you claim to know everything; at the same time as you tell me precisely, absolutely, nothing."

I had often spoken to him this rudely before; he had always seemed to enjoy it, indeed sometimes he'd encouraged me to. He asked mildly enough now what it was I wanted to know, and if I was sure I wanted to know it. But then left me so abruptly it was clear I had annoyed him. A moment later a vicious little wind got up. He's touchy as Lilith, I remember thinking as I wandered back towards our bower, letting the wind buffet me. Next day it was still blowing, but I was not concerned, quite the contrary, I welcomed the vigour and liveliness with which it seemed to drive out the discomforts of the evening, while I was exhilarated by the birds I saw making use of the wind's strong currents. In particular there was a flock of some kind of parrot, part-grey, part-rose colour, which soared and dived and fell in formation. When they turned their grey backs towards earth, they vanished simultaneously; when their pink breasts, they reappeared at once.

Beneath them on the plain the grasses flowed like water. I saw a whole meadow full of flowers rising and falling with the ebbing of the wind, like the fur on the back of an animal when it is stroked the wrong way; as they rose their scents too rose to my nostrils and fell away again, reminding me of something— though, tantalised, I could not tell what precisely, any more than I knew that from now on, from this first loss of my innocence, this undermining of my trust, I would always be longing for something I did not yet know or could not quite remember, afraid at the same time of I did not know quite what.

PART TWO

GIRL

Chapter One

Adam brought me many gifts in Eden. The serpent only ever gave me one. I'm pretty sure he meant it as a gift. It was so unlike any fruit I had encountered before that at first I even thought he had carved rather than grown it.

It was not a mistake I would usually have made. Yet I remained confused on that morning of all mornings, after Adam and I and Lilith had met together for the first time, after the wind had begun to blow; the morning the serpent told me his first story and everything began to change very quickly, or rather, in the arousing of my suspicions, I began to notice that it did.

Still watching the grasses flow, I had not heard the serpent come to me. I turned suddenly to find him at my back, holding out his fruit, with a look on his face, in his eyes—how yellow they were this morning—that puzzled me more than his usual ambiguous expression. Yet I could not mistake the nod by which he asked me to accept the gift he offered. Such a solid and heavy fruit it seemed, that I felt reluctant to take it in my hands. In the end, with an impatient shift of his eyes and golden fingers, he thrust it at me, rather rudely I thought, as I stroked the shallow ridges that defined the fruit's sides. Bending my eyes to this apparent globe, in order to avoid the serpent's gaze, I was surprised to find that it had no less than seven faces, while its grainy yellow skin, flushed pink in places, was so shiny and smooth the serpent might have lacquered it over. Not even the dried calyx of the flower standing at the top of the fruit, or the remains of dried stamens this contained, could entirely convince me that its origins were natural.

"What is it?" I asked the serpent curiously, as soon as I had thanked him.

"Don't you know? I can't think why you don't. It's a pomegranate," he replied, almost shyly; rolling the word round his tongue much as I rolled the fruit around between my hands. Indeed it had just the same pleasant gravity and weight.

"Why not taste it?" he added. "I think you'll find it delicious." But then, giving me no time to reply, he took the fruit firmly out of my hands, cut the calyx precisely in half and slit the fruit open with his sharp knife, releasing its sweet, yet tart, faint yet overwhelming scent into the air about us.

Nothing in Eden had ever seemed as new and strange as this. Maybe it was all those seeds—more seeds, apparently, than flesh—and in such intricate array; each seed contained by a juicy pink membrane, each group of seeds, ranged within fibrous segments inside the circumference of the fruit, as random, as ordered, as multiple as stars. For a moment I could not make head or tail of what I saw; indeed thought rather longingly of the simple five-pointed star formed by the seeds of an apple the serpent had cut open once. Why, on this morning of all mornings, I found myself wondering ungratefully, why *couldn't* he have brought me an apple instead of this over-complicated fruit?

The serpent was now asking in an offended voice why I had not yet tasted his gift. "I thought you could break your fast on it," he added, more patiently, yet as if the patience pained him. "I thought that one way and another you might have forgotten to eat this morning." And he was right, for the first time I had forgotten, as had my husband, Adam. Staring straight at him, till he turned his eyes away (shamefacedly was it—for what reason could he be ashamed?—how did he know I had not felt like eating?)—I picked out some seeds and crunched them between my teeth, letting the pink juice trickle down my tongue. I found it not at all an unpleasant taste, not especially distinctive; yet not quite like anything I'd ever tasted before.

These days I'm resigned, mostly, to such explosions of growth. What confuses me much more is the story I am trying to tell. It's been so simple till this point; at least I've known what needed to be said. But now, suddenly, as I began struggling to expose the taut yet golden thread that defines both my tale and myself, it feels like beating my head against a wall I can never breach; against the wall of the garden itself, perhaps, which keeps me enclosed within my ignorant innocence long after I've outgrown it.

Where to go next? Shall I move on to the stories the serpent began to tell the day he gave me the pomegranate? Or shall I return to the desert, to the events that made me acknowledge, finally, the nature of the fruit I chose to eat? It's quite time I did. Yet I find myself strangely reluctant, though nothing in Eden makes sense unless I try. What, at the very least, is the point of revealing the skills the serpent gave me in Eden if I do not show the uses I put them to? In the garden they remained simply interesting tricks. In the desert, on the other hand, they enabled us first to survive and then, ultimately, to flourish—indeed how often during those lonely days after I was raped by Sammael, I'd found myself blessing my old friend the serpent.

I blessed him when, missing Adam's animal warmth, I whittled out my firesticks with a flint and slowly and painfully made a fire to sit by through the bitter nights. I blessed him as I constructed my shelters against the sun and winds alike, and as I planted a few hard-won seeds, the forerunner of many other gardens I planted in more prosperous years to come. My child quickening in my womb, I blessed him even when my will to survive grew so fierce I began trapping some of the smaller animals and cooking them on my fires.

Later, while eating, I would apologise to brother lizard or sister rat or starling. For I still felt them to be my brothers and sisters and felt it all the more because of their gift of nourishment. Not that they could be expected to see it like that; not with the smell of roasting flesh floating across the desert for the first time in the history of the world. At night, though drawn to my fire, they would be careful to keep their distance. It made me lonelier than ever to see their eyes gleaming green or yellow, to hear in the enormous silence the sound of their breathing, their scurries and scufflings and the slow padding of much larger paws.

*

In Eden it was Lilith, of course, who had taught me what it meant to be a woman; in the same way that later all women would instruct their daughters and their sisters. She had not only demonstrated and named the emotions between men and women, between women and women, she named all the female functions and parts of our bodies also, clitoris and vulva, womb and cervix, so on and so forth. If the purpose of some of them—as indeed the purpose of many emotions—made no sense to me as yet, at the very least seemed eccentric, none, I realised, could be named or had been named by Adam; most he did not know existed, and if he did, he no more understood them than I understood them, before our expulsion from Eden, before Cain was conceived.

But I understood afterwards, all right. I reflected often on such matters, apprehensively, during those lonely yet strangely contented days in the desert when my baby grew inside me, and my navel—I had a navel I assure you—leapt out boldly from my belly, its crannies stretched and open to the world. At night the child beat so furiously within that I could not sleep. I began to long for his birth after a while. Yet having given up all hope of seeing Adam again, this lively baby was my only companion and I was more alarmed than grateful when I felt his antics quieten, just as I was bewildered by the surge of energy I felt very shortly. I used it though, as best I could, first building a hasty shelter, then gathering up a store of roots and preparing a new firestick. It was while I was whittling away, resting the wood on my extended belly, that my birth pains began.

I did not think much of them at first being so used to pain by now, to all kinds of pricks and tears and burns and bruises. I was familiar with the steady thump of an ache in the head and the jerks and throbs of over-used muscles. But that was random pain; this pain soon proved itself quite different—like the endlessly changing intervals between night and day; like the beating of my heart.

Of course I knew something about birth, not only in my body and senses; in the garden, before I knew it had anything to do with me, I knew that cats gave birth and cows and sheep and horses. I had even seen one birth, though I had not wholly understood what I was seeing. Despite which, and despite Lilith's teaching, I knew it like a beast, now I came to it, in my womb and belly rather than in my head; and therefore responded like a beast, without thought, instinctively, my fear the sort that knows certainty, not the more arbitrary kind. Panting and moaning I closed my eyes against the sun and sky, as if against the pain itself.

The earth turned very slowly at first. Between spasms I walked about, unwilling to take to my shelter yet. There was nothing but spiny bushes and thorn trees in that place, some with the kinds of roots that might hold water; these I had already noted, very carefully. Others provided a little shade; against the trunk of the best of them I'd constructed the shack in which my baby was to be born, open—I wanted it open—to the sun and earth and sky and my own deep womb alike. I was wringing wet now from head to foot. I crouched with my knees apart, feeling the scrape of the thorn bark against my back, and watched, disbelievingly, as the sweat rolled off me and soaked the earth around where I sat.

I do not know how long this lasted; all day, perhaps. With every hour the moaning intensified, the pain grew more over-whelming. It was not till suddenly it became confused and jumbled, beginning and stopping, starting and ending without rhythm or pattern, that the screams began. They were sharper than the sun, sharper than the thorns, sharper than the million, million grains of sand I felt beneath my body, every grain glittering, jabbing into me, containing as many colours as the burning rays of the sun. The screams stole my voice—how could they have been my voice—they stole, uttered shamelessly all my anger and hate. I cursed Lilith and Sammael; the serpent and Jehovah; above all I cursed Adam who had abandoned me to this.

An age of screams; an age of curses—wherever had I learned such words? Until, exhausted, I cursed no one any more. I felt a parting, a bearing down in the earth and sky; I was pushed down by the firmament, sucked down by the earth, a whole universe, a globe was being dragged out of me or I was being dragged out of it. My body in either case was as if splitting apart. I panted like a beast; soon I began screaming again, healthy, necessary screams this time.

I had been alone. Now I was not alone. I do not know precisely when Adam came, the exact stage at which I felt his hand on my forehead, smoothing away my hair that was matted with sweat and fear. Then both his hands were holding my two shoulders, and behind my moans and pants a voice ran, encouraging me, until the waves opened and opened, the world itself split and vomited me out; the blood and water flooding out from between my legs, I felt against my thighs a small, bony circumference, and heard a cry too thin and high to be my own.

The next moment the baby, the first of those miracles for which paradise had to be surrendered, lay on my belly, and the world was still, its convulsions once more beyond sense, inaudible.

Over and over I asked Adam why he'd come back, I remember. But he did not answer, any more than he'd used to answer questions in the garden if he could help it. Instead, clumsily, tenderly, with a sharp stone, he began severing the cord that joined me and my baby—heaven knows what instinct told him to do that. But so he did, then handed the baby to me. When I put it to my breast it sought for the nipple vainly, until I guided its mouth to the place.

"You know he's not your son; you know he's Sammael's bastard," I insisted weakly, not sparing my words, because I was determined, despite my exhaustion, not to let Adam cling to some illusion, even if it meant he might leave me again and I'd have to rear the baby alone. But all I did, it seemed, was hurt him, the way he looked at me and again, dumbly, shook his head. I should never have recognised him. Gaunt and dirty enough before he went away he was now nothing but bone, apart from the most meagre covering of skin, while his eyes burned out from a thicket of filthy hair and he had lost at least three teeth. I could smell him too, an acid smell, sharp as an animal's, compounded of sweat and pain and hunger and loneliness.

"So why did you come?" I insisted, for the last time. The tears were rolling down my cheeks by now, but still he would not answer me, merely touched my wet eyes and trembled violently, his eyes darting from side to side like the eyes of the wild beast whose skin he wore round him.

At that I put up my arms and he laid his head upon my breast, thereby at last acknowledging his weakness. They lay one on either side, Sammael's furious and already greedy child and Adam my new-made man and husband, who would have suckled too, I think, if he could, but did not know how to, that son of earth not flesh, or did not dare to. The baby, on the other hand, snuffling and gulping, clamped his mouth upon my nipple so hard he bruised me with his toothless gums, then fell to steady sucking.

Chapter Two

Lilith had used such bitter words once, as we wandered in the garden, to describe her own lost children, condemned by God as demons, she said, to die at their birth. Often, then as now, I'd find myself musing upon them, in sad bewilderment.

She'd asked, I remember, "Why should I be made to copulate with demons and give birth to other demons, merely because I prefer my own company? And why should I be hated for it? *Someone* has to copulate with demons; someone has to give birth to demons."

Later she had added, "It's all very well for you, Eve. You'll nurse your children, you'll suckle them. They'll take your milk and nothing but your milk. My children, on the other hand, will dig their teeth into my nipples and draw blood."

I had not known what she meant at the time. In particular, I had not known what she meant by the word "children", let alone, given the way she used it, what a glorious, not to say miraculous word it was. I did not know that morning when the same word came up in the first story the serpent told me. (Nibbling thoughtfully, meanwhile, upon my pomegranate seeds, I remained unaware, besides, that this strange new art he'd started to reveal, this story telling, was not only as dangerous and necessary as fire, but also the one I'd soon long for above the rest.) "Today, Eve," the serpent had begun—naturally I did not know what was coming; I'd been intending rather, in the hope of reassurance, to confess my indefinable unease after seeing Adam with Lilith— "Today, Eve, I propose to tell you a story about a man who built a boat."

He confused me at once since I had never heard the word "story" before, let alone the word "boat".

This man it seemed, much less virtuous than Adam, had lived in a land of men who weren't virtuous either, but a good deal more stupid—they did not think it worth their while to be polite to God; our hero did, on the other hand. Consequently, when God grew tired of all the quarrelling and misbehaviour, though he decided to get rid of his world and its inhabitants, he let himself be persuaded to make an exception of this cunning friend and his family and a few selected animals. (The man selected the animals; he did not, said the serpent with a sly look, include a snake.)

"Make a boat," God instructed the man tersely. Neither the man nor his wife nor his children were willing or skilful workers. But they set to work speedily when they heard how soon the rain would begin to fall and how long it would go on falling. As it did for more days and nights than they could count; till all the world was covered with water, and they, safe if not snug in their crude vessel, watched, with smug horror, the corpses of their drowned fellows drifting by. The rain stopped at last. The flood dried up. In due course these sailors, inept to the last, ran their boat aground upon a mountain, and having freed such animals as they had not eaten, went on with life much as before. The man took the precaution of continuing to pray to God, but no one else did. Who knows whether God regretted saving him?

That was the gist of the serpent's tale more or less, though it's always possible I've forgotten some part of it or even failed to see where the tale could be leading. After all there was almost nothing in it that did not puzzle me utterly, not least the fact that this man and his family existed; Adam was the only man so far as I knew.

I soon gave up, I remember, and abandoning my pointless questions, just opened my mind as to music, to a seductive melody, perhaps, or some stirring or disturbing rhythm, and let myself be dazzled. The serpent after all had often dazzled me before. No doubt he would dazzle me again, in this way as in all the rest.

In which I was right, of course. I also think that even from the beginning I saw more danger there than most. Unable to identify it, however, I chose—and seemed for the moment able—perhaps I had no alternative—to remain as oblivious to the danger as I was to the warnings with which the serpent's stories were loaded. Today's story had concerned the wrath of God for instance, but by the time he left me that afternoon I had quite forgotten it, not letting myself be reminded even when I heard Jehovah's relentless greeting.

Jehovah, of course, did not come to me till my amazement had almost subsided; not till long after I had devoured every seed from the pomegranate, every shred of flesh, spitting out only the bitter fibres, and leaving the empty shards lying on the ground where the heat immediately began to shrivel them. With no trace left, apparently, of this morning's wind, it had turned into such a very pleasant evening that I sat myself down on an inviting rock and basked in the rays of the late sun. Soon I began to feel that the world had put itself to rights; that I had imagined my confusions, invented all my longings and suspicions. By the time Jehovah spoke to me I was already half-asleep, never supposing, even remembering the vicious little wind he'd raised, that I had any need to be careful of what I said and did in his presence. In reply to his greeting, I proclaimed, rather cheekily, "Oh it's you again is it? Am I never to be left in peace?"

At which he laughed and I felt easier than ever. In any case, I could hardly have been more innocuously employed, lying somnolent and comfortable upon my warm rock and basking in the late sun. If I fondled my body here and there it was only for the pleasure of it—I fondled myself between my legs no less than the rest, since I'd never yet felt the need to be bashful about any part of my anatomy. The sensation it gave me being particularly pleasant, I let my hand lie in that place a longer time than most.

Indeed I am still not entirely certain why I did start feeling bashful. Jehovah had been asking another harmless enough question about the evening with Lilith and Adam; I might have had reason to be annoyed by this since I was at this moment attempting to forget it, yet I had no reason to feel embarrassed. All the same I did begin to find myself embarrassed—even a little ashamed. Perhaps I'd remembered Lilith murmuring, "Oh what a sexy little thing you are," the last time I'd fondled myself in front of her. Yet it wasn't Lilith's voice in my head but my own that made me remove my hand abruptly and pretend it had been attending to some less intimate affair.

Immediately there was silence in the garden. I concluded I'd been left alone again, until Jehovah's voice asked quietly—in such a different tone that it seemed to come from outside me instead of from inside my head as usual—why I had sat up so suddenly; why, indeed, I was blushing?

"I am not blushing," I lied, confusedly. To prove it I picked a small purple flower that grew beside the rock. But on my crushing the petals between my fingers it gave off, to my further shame and embarrassment, a scent which reminded me of Adam when he made love to me.

Even so, I could not imagine why Jehovah proceeded to ask, very quietly, if I had by any chance been nibbling a forbidden fruit. I did not understand the question at first; he had to rephrase it before I realised that by forbidden fruit he meant the figs from the tree of knowledge and of death.

"They're not ripe yet," I answered indignantly, and was taken aback to hear Jehovah enquire how I knew the figs weren't ripe, had I been to look at them? Protesting, too speedily, that I didn't need to, you could see the trees from the other side of the river, I proceeded to entangle myself still further, while the voice continued to goad me, sadly, implacably, even viciously at times. Ever more confused and annoyed I heard myself saying at last, "I'll have to eat your wretched fruit for the hell of it, if you must talk to me like this."

I don't think I meant my words the least seriously. Judging, however, by the iciness of the silence that followed and the even icier voice in which at last Jehovah broke it, he took what I said very seriously indeed. And by doing so you could say it was he himself, God forbid, who first put into my head the still inconceivable notion that it would be possible for me to disobey his law.

Jehovah went away then, taking with him my peace of mind and leaving behind an evening no longer easy, racked by savage little winds. Trembling, I stayed leaning against a sweet chestnut tree, watching the clouds pile up like cliffs. Their edges were fire colour, so bright sometimes I could scarcely look at them, though their centres remained as black as night. The winds fell silent for a while, everything became dangerously still. Then sudden small gusts began whiffling the leaves above my head—I felt them in my hair and on my body, and when I glanced up saw more wind tearing towards me across the meadow. The flowers and grasses looked as if they would be torn out by their roots, while leaves were blowing past me in their hundreds, leaves, it seemed, from every kind of tree that grew in the garden. I was terrified at the sight, yet no less excited—I wanted the wind to catch and take me too, so driving out of me the memory of the evening. At the same time I clung to my tree with all my strength, feeling its bark scrape against my body, snuffing up its oddly carnal scents. When would it start to rain? I wondered, the clouds growing blacker than ever. For the first time I remembered the story the serpent had told me.

Hadn't the man in it faced an even mightier storm raised by Jehovah's wrath and hadn't it rained thereafter for many days and nights? Suppose it rained like that in Eden—suppose—but I didn't believe it, and very soon I began to long for rain. As darkness fell the wind howled ever louder, whipping the clouds faster and faster across the sky, before crashing them together, seemingly to make thunder and lightning; sheets and bolts of sound and light lit and battered the landscape all night, without any relief from water. Though I tried to make a shelter it proved impossible, my materials whipped away as fast as I gathered them, very soon I gave up, just crouched, whimpering, trying to protect myself from flying debris and watching the skies open and shut above my head, while I begged them over and over to let the rain fall. When Adam found his way to me at last, much later than usual, I flung myself into his arms and berated him for leaving me alone before such electric, arid fury.

★

Though the wind had died next morning and the sky cleared, the ground was still strewn with leaves, twigs and even branches; I had never seen such destruction. Hoping it was not all on my account, I felt lonely and longed for company. I longed for Lilith in particular, despite my memories of our last evening together. A figure in the distance did seem to be Lilith at first. I called her name, only to encounter the serpent, clearing up the debris and none too pleased to have been mistaken for my sister, especially since I could not hide my disappointed look. He seemed generally in melancholic mood; certainly he had no stories to tell. After we had worked together for a little while he softened enough to offer me an apple, which I refused—simply because I wasn't hungry—but he took it as an insult for some reason, and when I accused him of being as touchy as Lilith he turned, and with a hiss so prolonged and vicious it made me draw in my breath, said, "Lilith, Lilith. Why must I always hear about Lilith?"

"You hear no more of her than you hear of Adam," I said, trying to tease him a little, "who is my husband after all."

"And do you talk to them about me?" The serpent spoke slyly this time.

"Sometimes," I replied, looking at him guardedly. Though aware by now that such discussions were better avoided, I did not expect what I heard next—I did not even take it in at first, the serpent's voice was so bland and conversational.

"Well perhaps, Eve," he said, "perhaps the time has come for me to talk to you about them: Adam and Lilith."

"What is there to talk about?" I asked, coolly, taking the apple that he offered and raising it to my lips to hide my sudden fear.

"Does it not occur to you, Eve," he enquired with smooth venom before I could dig my teeth into it. "Does it *never* occur to you to wonder why, if those two have both been around so much longer than you have, why they had never met? *If* they have never met."

Giving me a sideways glance, he left the question in the air. And when, letting my apple fall untasted after all, I protested he could not put such ideas into my head and just leave it at that, merely asked, "What ideas?" in an interested voice; and suggested that I could always ask Adam about anything that puzzled me, or Lilith of course, though that might be the more dangerous procedure. Whereupon he looked at me directly and smiled for the first time, and I smiled too in an understanding of which I was at once ashamed since it seemed disloyal to my friend. The serpent bowed at this with another ironic look. Thereafter he put on a more pleasant expression than he had worn all morning and left me to my thoughts.

They were wild thoughts at first. I wandered aimlessly, at length found myself by the river. It seemed less overgrown these days than when I'd met Lilith there, I could see the trees of life and death across it. Though the current ran strongly, I plunged into the water, and having reached the other side found myself able to assess the progress of the fruit on the two trees quite dispassionately and calmly. The apples on the tree of life were twice the size already, almost their full size, I thought, and if they were still unripe, it couldn't be long before they were ready for Adam and me to eat.

The figs too remained green. But they had swelled considerably. And when, in an act of defiance (for I had been overtaken by unexpected waves of anger against the serpent, Adam, Lilith, Jehovah, all of them) I reached out and touched the nearest one, the flesh did seem to give a little beneath my fingers; if so it was not significant, not yet. I *told* Jehovah they were unripe, I thought indignantly.

Chapter Three

It was a day or two still before I could bring myself to mention my suspicions either to Lilith or Adam. Much as I brooded, wandering alone, the moment I met my husband or my sister I seemed able to dismiss my fears from my mind—probably I did not dare to mention them, in case what the serpent had hinted turned out to be true. And what I wanted above all was for it not to be true; for things to be exactly as they had always seemed.

It was so, I remember, the day that Lilith and I were to find the serpent's knife; the day our jealousy surfaced, exacerbated by her seemingly wilful behaviour. Pushing away as usual my memories of that uncomfortable evening, with Adam and of what the serpent had hinted, I'd said nothing to her at first about my feelings. Indeed, after an affectionate if wary greeting, neither of us spoke much. We sat making daisy chains under a conker tree, the meadow in front of us gentle compared to some other places in Eden; even the colours in its lush grass seemed muted.

Everywhere—across the meadow, on the trees and bushes at its borders—flowers and leaves alike were beyond full bloom, brown-edged in places, almost drooping. Yet the effect was not melancholy. In their decay I saw perhaps the same reassuring vulnerability that I saw in Lilith herself. Her very laugh seemed hushed, her glitter had mellowed to a tolerable glow. The lines around her eyes were as plain as the veins on the leaves that drifted to our feet from the tree above our heads.

For a long while she lay, her head pillowed in my lap, while I, with careful fingernail, continued to penetrate the stalks of the small white-petalled flowers. By threading each head through the stalk of another I'd been able to make her necklaces and bracelets.

I'd started on a crown for her head, when I found myself asking, idly enough, why she so rarely sneezed these days when she had used to sneeze so very frequently.

Lilith replied that her nose must have grown unaccustomed to such highly scented places, after being away from them so long.

"And is it used to the garden now?" I asked.

"For the moment," she replied.

"You mean you might start sneezing again," I teased her. "And what happens when you do?" But I knew one answer even before she made it, and as I did so might have felt a cooler breeze upon my cheek—maybe Lilith had just moved apart a little.

"Do you think it might be wise of me to go away again?" she asked. Now she was teasing me, so disarmingly, however, I was only afraid for a moment, and thereafter plied her with questions too light-heartedly to take them seriously myself, even when I began putting some of those I'd recently kept phrasing in my head but somehow never got round to asking.

How many of the animals had she met, for instance, during her first stay in the garden, I demanded without fear or guile. (Oh yes, conkers were falling from the tree above our heads, but they did not fall near us and where they hit the ground their armoured husks broke open, always, to show the polished nuts inside.)

"I met some of them, of course. Perhaps most of them."

"The serpent?" I broke in eagerly.

"Oh yes, certainly the serpent. But what I suppose you really want to know is whether I encountered Adam?"

She took the words from my mouth, more or less; with terror and even shame I discovered where the conversation was leading. Trembling I completed my final daisy chain—she had barely let me set it round her neck before she laughed, cried impatiently, "Enough—that's enough." The next moment she'd leapt up and pulled me to my feet.

"Come on," she cried, "come on," and began running across the meadow. She was laughing when she looked back at me running after her, but I, my questions suddenly as desperate as before they had been casual, was begging her breathlessly, "Tell me Lilith, tell me did you meet Adam ever?"

"Of course," she shouted back—she did not seem to be out of breath at all. "How could I not have met him?" She had already reached the far side of the meadow. Instead of waving grass we were surrounded by thickets of prickly bushes, on which pinkish flowers were being replaced by fruit that was almost ripe in places, turning everywhere from green to red to black.

"Why did you never tell me?" I was demanding. I took her by the shoulders, meant only to wait for her answer before ripping the daisy necklaces from her and pushing her back among the thorns. In my terror and bewilderment there's no doubt I would have done these things or tried to, had my eye not been caught by a flash of steel from the ground, half-hidden by grasses. Lilith saw it simultaneously. As we bent down to look more closely, she said, almost under her breath, but mirthfully, "But Eve, you never asked." At that moment, precisely, we discovered the serpent's knife.

My hand reached it first. Lilith's lips parted when I thrust the knife towards her. All questions momentarily driven from my mind, I saw her stare at it with an expression of loathing and longing—then she snatched it from me and held it in her hand, running a finger along its blade so much more delicately than I had once managed to that no blood appeared on her skin. The knife seemed less exotic than it did when the serpent held it, yet even more dangerous. Indeed its sharp gleam and vicious edge were being taken on by Lilith visibly as I watched. Her eyes had grown sharp as needles. Her vivacity was marvellous—I didn't know which of them, she or the knife, was more alien in that place, but I observed their alienness with grief and pain because it meant I'd lose her in the end, whatever became of us; and worse, in my jealousy, I even felt glad of it.

She was wreathing the knife about her now, darting and dashing it, its little glitters fearful in the mellow afternoon light. They reminded me of Adam's fireflies except that it was daylight and they did not dance aimiably, as the fireflies had danced.

What next, I was thinking, what next, and heard Jehovah saying, *I told you so*, smugly. "But what *have* you told me, save riddles?" I screamed back. Like a charm to ward off evil—a

particularly desperate charm—I found myself shouting aloud—
no, bellowing, "Lilith, I love you." Meaning, "I hate you."
Adding beneath my breath, "Why did you lie about Adam?
Why? Why? Why?"

(It was then, from the corner of my eye, I caught a quiver in the
long grass. More than a quiver—as I turned my head I seemed to
glimpse a figure there running away from us—Adam, who
else?—very bent and furtive—in a moment it was gone and I
thought I had imagined it; in another moment I had forgotten it
altogether.)

"Ah but I love you too, Eve," Lilith was hissing meanwhile. I'd barely looked back at her before the knife flickered
towards me—I heard a snick, snick, beside my ear; at once she
was holding aloft a strand of my hair.

With a crow of laughter she shouted, "And now I've something to remember you by, Eve. And here's something for you to
remember me by when I'm gone."

I put out my hand to take the lock she cut from herself and gave
me. One moment I almost had her, the next she'd broken away
and was running to and fro among the grasses, among the thorny
bushes, the blade flashing around her; from each flash sprang up a
flower, a thorn, a leaf. Sometimes whole sprays, whole branches,
were severed, the earth behind her was littered wherever she
went.

I had never seen that knife used for purposeless destruction
before; soon she was spinning it and herself so fast I scarcely saw
the blade except as a gleam and a shimmer, saw only the flowers
and berries leaping and falling; if she made me feel giddy where I
stood, what did she feel like, I wondered? She was swaying
drunkenly, dipping and turning, her arms whipping hither and
thither. The flash and flicker of light, ever quicker and brighter,
so dazzled and confused me, I turned my head away. The peals of
laughter she flung across the meadow had become more like
shrieks now of pain or delight—I was beginning to think I could
not endure them any more when they grew to a crescendo and
died away altogether. At the same moment, slowly, even
gracefully, Lilith subsided to the ground. I did not move. I

watched her and waited. At last, still slowly, she rose to her feet and began to move towards me, slower than ever, languorous even, but not panting as I would have expected after her wild exertions. As soon as she was near enough she handed me the knife.

"Now you can use it any way you want," she told me, giving a derisive smile. "Even on me if you choose to. Even on yourself."

I knew and did not know exactly what she meant. All the same I did not want the knife any longer. I shifted it from palm to palm, feeling how hot it was and how damp with her sweat. Her hands too were still hot and moist when she placed them upon my shoulders, but, her smile derisive no longer, she gave me as near an apologetic look as she was capable of giving.

"The serpent always did make clever tools," she said.

"Yes. He does," I replied, so exhausted suddenly there remained but the faintest shadow of my new-born hate.

"And I suppose he shows them to you one by one and makes you more and more inquisitive. You had better be careful, Eve, he's very clever."

"No more clever than you," I said reluctantly. Lilith neither confirmed nor denied this. She continued giving me a look I could not endure, at the same time as I could not read it. At last, in desperation, I cast the knife down so fiercely the blade penetrated the earth. It stood quivering for a moment—when I moved to pick it up again, Lilith drew me back and, her voice kinder now, urged, "No don't, Eve; leave it; he'll find it when he wants."

"You mean the serpent?"

"Who else, my dearest little ninny."

I found myself passionately wishing he would not, but chose not to say so. Lilith was sighing in any case, as if she too had forbidden all further questions. In a moment, to my surprise and unease, she sneezed once, discreetly, before turning and walking away across the meadow, all the lightness gone from her step; indeed she looked so disconsolate, even sad suddenly, that I ran after, wanting only to comfort her, made too conscious of how the distances were closing in now for evening, the flowers breathing out all their heavy scents, to take in fully the fearful certainties I'd learned that afternoon. No less than that the world was not always to be trusted; that my friends could lie to me—and what was worse they had, and worse still that everyone in the garden had known it except me from the moment I'd emerged into its penetrating light.

That night, for the first time since I had emerged from Adam's body, he did not come to find me. I slept alone and lonely in the open air, having no heart to make myself a shelter, though for once I would have welcomed one. I awoke frequently, imagining I heard his step; but he never came, while I asked myself over and over where he could have got to. I did not, in Eden, think he'd come to any harm. But remembering the way I'd seen him look at Lilith it occurred to me to wonder—I writhed at the thought—if he could have gone to her side instead of mine. I dismissed the thought with difficulty by reminding myself firmly that he wasn't married to Lilith. And it was only towards dawn that I remembered again what the emotions of the afternoon had wiped from my mind, the brief image I had had of Adam fleeing through the grass. Perhaps it wasn't an illusion. Perhaps I really had seen him. But then what was he doing spying on us both? And why, oh why should he want to run away from me?

At which painful thought I fell asleep. And awoke at full daylight to find myself enfolded in Adam's passionate embrace. In my relief and joy at his return, I had but one question left to ask him. "Adam where were you?" I did not even find it hard to believe his answer; he had wandered too far to reach me before dusk, he said, so had slept where he was, hurrying to my side at the first light of dawn.

Chapter Four

I can think of several good reasons why the serpent had started to tell me his stories at this time. It was a means, for instance, not only of diverting me, but of pulling my thoughts outside the garden where he wanted them to go; where all his other teaching was taking me, if only I had known. That way he captivated me since no one else thought to amuse me in such a fashion. At the same time I think he could not help himself; there was no one else to whom he could pass on his art—both Lilith and Adam were too busy in their heads, while Adam, at least, was too afraid. And he did seem to need to pass on his arts.

At about the same time, for instance, that he started telling me his stories he taught me to mould vessels from the clay, baking them in a fire to make them watertight. This story telling art—just one among the rest—or so he made it seem—he gave me that too, though at first only by persuading me that there were stories to be told; it was not until later it became clear that my story was one of them.

Storytelling was also, of course, a means of forestalling questions he preferred not to answer. When I met him that morning after leaving Adam he must have observed the remains of my agitation. Before I could open my mouth he said with smooth haste, "Today, Eve, I'll tell you about a tall tower." And in a moment I was enthralled; alternately I was scared or exhilarated, uneasy or bemused—played on as if I were an instrument, I had to respond to him even where I did not understand a word. He dwelt particularly lovingly, for example, when describing the tower to me, on what he called the details of its construction and engineering; a difficult matter as far as I was concerned, since the rough shelters he and I had made could hardly be described as building and that was the only construction that I knew.

But what puzzled me still more was the climax of the story when the builders climbed so high they forgot how to speak to the people who lived on the ground, just as the people who lived on the ground forgot how to speak to them. How could one person fail to understand the words of another? I wondered. After a while I even asked the serpent, jokingly, if he would speak to me in a language I didn't know, not believing he'd be able to. But having been merry enough till now, telling his tale to lively, dramatic effect, he turned serious suddenly and gave me a warning and sardonic look.

"Do you really want to know such things?" he asked. "Would it not be wiser to leave well alone?"

But I said nothing, just stared at him relentlessly; until at last he shook himself and embarked on a series of hissing syllables which made no sense whatever and which turned him into a dangerous stranger, whose suspicious, even vicious glances I might read, on the other hand, in any way I chose.

At once he made as if to depart. I was glad on the whole—though relieved, a little, to hear him call over his shoulder, "I'll soon have something to show you Eve," in words I understood. But then, to my alarm, he turned back suddenly and having regarded me intently for a moment, he seized my hand and said, "Or now, if you like. If you insist on it."

Immediately he set off at such a breakneck speed I needed too much breath for keeping up with him to be able to ask where he was taking me. In any case I almost did not want to know. I suspected that some of his secrets were fearful—at the very least they might divide me from my husband. Maybe at this moment I felt relieved to be divided from him; yet I did not dare to believe it, not even when we advanced into such steep and stony country, so difficult to walk in it became clear I was leaving everything I knew behind and that most likely neither Adam nor Lilith could follow me.

★

The serpent had dropped my hand by now. But he would still offer me his on occasions where the going became particularly hard, offering me too some charming yet rather detached smiles from which I would turn my head. For once he did not seem inclined to take offence. He did not even seem to care much whether I took his hand or not, though when I did his cool dry skin touched mine confidently without flinching. But I was not inclined to keep hold of him any longer than I had to and sometimes rejected his help altogether, jumping down or pulling myself up rock faces unassisted.

We crossed a stream or two; mostly irritable waters hustling over stones, but occasionally deep pools where ferns had fitted themselves into crevices in their stone walls, some pendant, some upright. They were very green ferns, often glittering with water. There were flowers too in places, their petals shiny, their leaves upright like spears or knives, and above these striped insects were darting. Higher still flew small birds like jewels; indeed everything, ferns, flowers, insects, birds, even the blue sky beyond the sheer cliffs and crags, had a fixed, bright, metallic quality—just as the trickle of water came to my ears with the precise quality of the sound made by the serpent's knife when he chipped it against a stone.

We stopped by one pool and drank at my request. Afterwards the serpent put a hand on my shoulder and stroked it briefly, though awkwardly. By this time the mystery of the place and of our journey had so disarmed me that I did not resist him, for all the questions that still remained unasked.

"It's not much further," he said, reassuringly, before I had spoken.

"I'm not tired," I protested.

"Did I say you were? Though you may be tired yet. For soon, dear Eve, the secret heart of all my skills is to be revealed to you. I hope you will appreciate how privileged you are, what power I offer if you will only choose to use it."

"That's a conceited way of putting it," I replied mechanically, in no mood for such banter. For banter was what it seemed in such a place, surmounted by jagged pinnacles of rock. Feeling for the first time a total stranger to myself as well as to my husband and sister, I did not dare believe him. Yet nothing now would have stopped me going on. I responded quite meekly when the serpent insisted we keep on climbing though my calves and thighs very soon began to ache.

At last we came to a rocky valley set high among the hills. All plant life ceased at its entrance. There were two caves facing each other in its barren walls, and closer at hand a crude structure made of stone, reminding me of the shelters the serpent had taught me to build, though it was taller and the walls did not give to my touch. Smoke crept from a hole in the roof and from between interstices in the stone. Not knowing what made smoke or even what it was, I assumed the stones and the roof gave off this misty substance, indeed for a moment I suspected that they themselves were moving.

There was a door at one side of the building; through it billowed more smoke; deep within I caught sight of an intense white glow. I could feel its terrible heat from several yards away, but I was not afraid of it—quite the reverse—the fire drew my eyes and my desire. What frightened me rather was the stillness of the valley. For there was no sound of water any more; not a bird, not an insect, not any sign of life except for the serpent standing motionless, his head thrust a little forward, his eyes staring unblinkingly into the hut, into the heart of the fire. Once he moved towards it—but only as far as the stone wall of the hut. There he bent for a moment, then held out to me a handful of pebbles, some dull, some glittering, but all of them coloured— white, blue, red, green or even purple. I had only seen colours like that on flowers before. How strange of stones, I thought, to take such colours on themselves.

The serpent did not let me hold his stones for long. He went inside the shelter and returned carrying larger, wholly opaque hunks of metal, white, yellow, reddish, one grey-blue like the blade of his knife and all faintly gleaming. As I touched each smooth surface with my fingers, I asked if they had names.

"Adam named them; as he names most things."

"He never told me about these," I said.

"Of course not. He does not approve of what I do to them. He does not even like them," said the serpent with an air of slight triumph. For he clearly liked them very much; he stroked each piece lovingly before handing it to me. What I felt, however, I did not know for sure. There was life in these substances certainly, but not a life I'd seen before. Why had he brought me to this place, I wondered? Was it because Adam did not like the arts it sheltered? I did like them on the other hand. I feared and marvelled equally, not least at the way the serpent had begun to look at me. He seemed to be beseeching me somehow, but I did not know what he wanted.

"Don't you want to know how I made them?" he asked at last. "How I dug the rough rock out of the earth? How I separate the metal in my furnace?"

"Perhaps," I said cautiously, "perhaps you had better show me." And so then he did, but I cannot begin to describe all of it; the way we crept ever deeper into the bowels of the earth, into a thick, muffled darkness quite different from the kind in which the stars were hung; the way I watched the serpent plunder the rock face; the way afterwards, in his blazing furnaces, he drained the bright substances from the dull rock.

But all the time I saw his assurance grow. When I stood with him beside his furnace, watching him feed it, he almost seemed part of it himself. The light catching his scales, they appeared to burn no less seriously than it burned, burning ever more brightly as he blew the flames higher till they became more like metal than flesh. Sometimes he would take a lump of the metal he had made, heat it on the fire, then lay it on a flat stone nearby and start hammering it into shape with a tool also made of some kind of metal. There were many such tools here, hung on hooks on the walls of the stone hut, or else scattered around, less delicate tools than his knife, but quite serviceable, I discovered, as he put them to use.

With one tool, shaped like the jaws of a wolf, he took metal from the fire, with another, more like the beak of a bird, he bore down on the metal and flattened it, with yet a third he wrenched and pulled it into whatever shape he wanted. He would hold the metal back in the fire from time to time. It would turn red first—as soon as it turned white he would take it out, and then to the smoke from the fire, the leaping flames, the shadows of the flames on the wall, the serpent's ever-moving body, would be added yet another mobile substance, noisier than most and hot too, I would discover as I set my hand to the hissing steam, snuffing up the hot, strong, almost animal smell of it.

Too absorbed to take notice of my fear, I was afraid, all the same. At times I even wondered if the serpent was Jehovah in another guise. For I could not imagine any God more splendid than this, with his broad shoulders and intently burning eyes, with his skilful hands manipulating red heat and white heat, hot metal and cold. At the same time he was writing his light and shade on my body. Growing hotter and hotter I wondered if he would be able to dissolve and reform me, too, in any way he liked, just as he did the gold and the silver, the copper and the iron.

I almost wanted him to dissolve me. I drew nearer and nearer the fire, the sweat streaming off my face—maybe, I thought, my flesh was dissolving already. The serpent laid aside for the moment the blade he had been working on. How huge he looked, waiting for me beside the fire, like a dark and fiery angel rather than one of the animals. I do not know which drew me more, his flesh or the fire—I put out a hand to each but met the serpent first. Though he had looked so hot he was cool to my touch, and jerked away, shuddering, only to bend his head forward almost at once and let me touch him again, allowing me to experience his resentment and his longing equally. Gradually as I stroked him and the untended fire quietened, his shuddering eased, he also quietened. Yet I did not stop, I went on stroking him, my fingers more and more alive to the meeting of one scale with another, to the invisible, unbearable sinuosities with which his flesh responded.

I was shuddering myself now. I did not know why. I did not know if I was glad he'd brought me here or regretted it bitterly. It did not matter very much. Regret or joy were equally meaningless as he whispered in my ear, "They were man and wife, you know, long ago, after Jehovah made them. And then she ran away into the desert. That's what you wanted to hear; that's why I had to bring you here so I could tell you. Not that I needed to. I think you knew already." And I nodded, because I did know, and also because I felt as if we were no longer in his stone hut, but deep inside the mountain, where such things were of no importance. So why had he told me here, I wondered? I had begun to draw my hands to and fro across his scales now, with a sense I drew metals from it, with a sense that he was the mountain, and that I was robbing him, shamelessly.

I think at that moment he could have kept me there with him for ever—perhaps he had been tempting me to stay when he told me about Adam and Lilith. Who knows how things might have turned out if I had? Jehovah would have had to change his plans for sure. But he did not keep me. Instead he began shuddering again. In due course, very gently, he put my hands from his flesh; we emerged at long last into daylight, blinking.

The valley seemed at the same time cool and gentle, unbearable and vast. The serpent was carrying an iron collar he had made, a beautiful thing, though quite without ornament. When he set it round my neck its chill weight appalled me, but before I could tear it off he himself removed it, shaking his head. I supposed that he would carry it with him just the same, but after hesitating a moment he laid it down upon a rock. Then he left it there behind us, and led me back down to green country, to my sister and my husband, to whatever else was to befall us.

Chapter Five

As if this had not been enough for one day, that same evening the serpent showed me how to make fire. Maybe he was still trying to keep my mind from other things—certainly this art proved a lengthy and tedious business. I was not allowed to practise his lively, flashy business with a knife and flint; instead he made me set one piece of wood in a groove that he'd gouged in another and spin it till I was weary and disheartened. It was only when I had it smouldering at last that I got round to making him repeat what he had told me while we were standing by his furnace.

I admit he did not want to do so. He kept insisting that anything he let slip when he was working did not matter anywhere else; I wouldn't like what he had to say, he added, and was much better off without it. All the same, I went on pestering him, until at last, shrugging, he reiterated the fact that in the beginning, before I had been made, Adam and Lilith were husband and wife. Then he went away offended, saying, "Don't say I didn't warn you," and it was true he had warned me; at the same time he had made it impossible for me to heed his warnings.

What I'd learned felt quite different from what I'd learned before. I clutched my smouldering firestick and trembled, the knowledge like a pebble in my mouth too big and cold to swallow. I was not angry this time, as at Lilith's revelation; I was frightened—so frightened, so very cold, that when my first firestick died I warmed myself by laboriously making another one, and used it to light a fire to sit by; the first fire I had made. It took a long time and ought to have been a triumph, and was, in a way. As I fed its little flames, I was saying to myself, blankly, defiantly, "Well then, so what? I can manage without any of you, look what I can do."

"Look what I can do," I shouted to the trees when no one answered. But they did not answer either, my defiance only brought the angels. As I huddled over the flames, warming my cold body, my even colder feelings, I looked up to see all four of them, Michael, Uriel, Gabriel, Raphael, standing above and around me, like trees with spreading branches, covered in spangled fruit.

They addressed me by turns and in their various ways—behind each angelic voice, however, I heard a mixture of fear and of triumph, more significant probably than the differences in what they said. Each one of them, for instance, told me my firemaking was not natural. Besides which Raphael warned that fires could all too easily get out of control, were therefore better not played with, while Uriel and Michael spoke a rather shrill hymn to Jehovah, their purpose to make me remember that only he, blessed be his name, was the source of such phenomena. (None of them could bring themselves to pronounce the word "fire"; it took me a while to understand that this was what they meant.) By apeing his powers, they said, I dishonoured his creation—Gabriel added that it was, moreover, ungrateful of me, implying that Jehovah had not provided sufficiently for my needs.

He was referring in particular, I think, to an apple dropped in the embers by mistake that I had taken out to find not only hot but malleable to my touch, its skin splitting in a couple of places. I nibbled at it cautiously, amazed to find its previously crisp flesh grown softer than the flesh of a mango or a peach. It was ironic, I suppose, even unkind, that the angels were unwilling spectators of the first cooking ever done; of my first, gritty, smoky taste of food heated in a fire. When, rather naughtily, I offered them a bite of it, they vanished at once.

It was dark already. The light of my disreputable fire defined an area around me, beyond which was an emptiness denser than usual. Dropping more apples into the embers I wondered where Adam was and whether he, too, would disapprove of my new skill. Not that I cared much if he did; I myself had good reasons to disapprove of him tonight; in fact I had every right to be furious. But I was not furious; I was still not angry in the least, just tired and puzzled and apprehensive and afraid.

When Adam came I saw, for the first time, dismayed, the extent of his fear where the serpent's arts were concerned. His eyes gleaming in the firelight like a wild animal's, he shied from the leaping of its flames and sat as far away from my fire as possible, never taking his eyes off it.

"Eve, Eve, what have you done?" he kept asking, the sweat running down his beard, down the hair on his chest. And though he bit tentatively into the hot apple I offered him, he spat it out at once with an exclamation of horror; then told me, more kindly and patiently—his patience clearly cost him some effort—that apples were better eaten the way they had grown. He did not, I was thankful, invoke the name of Jehovah; he made his objections out to be practical, even gastronomic ones. Yet he was governed by fear as clearly as the angels had been, if at the same time lacking their triumph. And when, grown impatient in my turn, I taxed him with his marriage to Lilith, he appeared more relieved by the change of subject than worried by its nature. He did not even seem to think the matter important, looking at me blankly as I protested at his deceit.

"Does it matter?" he said, at last. "I'm married to you now, Eve; what has Lilith to do with it?"

I did grow angry then, for a moment. "What do you think?" I shouted at him. But when he shook his head, my anger faded, my questions about his pretending not to know her became oddly subdued. He claimed to have made no such pretence; her behaviour had made him a stranger, as far as he was concerned, why should he have treated her in any other way? And if he'd deceived me thereby he was sorry, but on the whole he thought these matters were better left in the past and certainly better not revealed to me. Look, he said, at the fuss you are making now.

It did not seem as if we would ever understand one another. Was it really so simple for him as he made out? And though that was the end of the discussion for this evening—though we were exhausted—Adam insisted on waiting till the fire had died before he would make a bower, before he would let us sleep.

He woke up screaming in the night—he'd dreamed, he said, that my flames had been eating him. "Leave it alone, Eve, leave it alone," he begged me the next morning, the dream still lingering in his eyes. "Can't you see it is not for us? Can't you see it's not natural?"

So there it was again, that same word, natural; the one that Adam clung to, all the more fervently as the days went by. Having seen across the ages the worst things the serpent's arts can lead to, I understand better now why they should have frightened him so badly. Yet I do not regret my willingness to espouse them, any more than I regret passing such arts to my children.

I understand better, too, a disputation I heard about that time between Sammael and the serpent, on the merits of nature as opposed to culture (by which the serpent meant technology mainly; once, defiant of Eden, he even used that word). Sammael's defence of what he called the natural world was as passionate as Adam's but much more articulate; it might have impressed me more if he hadn't in practice so patently despised it—the natural world being Eden, the animals, Adam and myself—that he could scarcely bring himself to gaze on a single part of it. Indeed he based one whole section of his argument on the assumption that a trunk to a tree was as a skeleton to an animal, ignoring the serpent's protest that men and animals were constructed quite differently.

Not that the serpent's defence of culture could wholly be trusted either, since he defined as cultural everything his own skill had created—from his mining of metals to agriculture—that is his cultivation of the garden. If things can be improved on why shouldn't they be? was the basis of his reasoning.

"Is it natural to let a tree wither?" he had asked, I remember, "when by diverting a river round it, you can make it live longer?"

"Is it unnatural," I addressed both the angels and Adam in my head, "Is it unnatural to let an apple fall in the embers?—God told us to enjoy the fruits of the earth—he never tells us to enjoy them in one way, not another."

I questioned Lilith on the subject when I met her next morning. And was immediately treated to a dissertation abstruse enough not to have shamed Sammael. I suspected her of teasing me. I suspected her, also, more seriously, of diversionary tactics since this way she kept me from broaching some more awkward subjects. In the end, crudely, I conjoined the two and asked her straight out which term, natural or cultural, she'd use to describe her marriage to Adam.

"Natural, of course, in the beginning," she replied. "We were the only man and woman in the garden, our bodies complementary, our desires already implanted. Later—well maybe you could say we developed some kind of domestic culture, but not a successful one. . . . Of course . . ." Here she paused, however and looked at me curiously.

"So you know," she said. "Well you were bound to know some time. Not that I should let it worry you. Nature, you could say, got things all wrong in our case. Besides it isn't important any longer."

"How can it have been unimportant? You say so, Adam says so, but I simply don't believe it. If it was unimportant, why did you say nothing?"

"Because it was unimportant. And because it has nothing to do with you, little girl."

Her tone was dangerous for a moment. I did not care in the slightest. "What I want to know is," I said obstinately, "if Adam was married to you, why did he need me? Why ever was I *made*?"

Which was the crux of the matter, of course, if I could not yet see it. Lilith, who knew better, regarded me steadily, the mocking glint that came and went in her eyes belied by the gravity with which she asked, "Do you want me to repeat to you the whole tedious story?"

"It is not tedious to *me*," I cried, maddened by her evasions.

"Then do you think you are in a state to hear it?"

We were high up in a valley somewhere at the time, a place

only a little less rocky than the one I'd visited yesterday, though this time I'd wandered there alone, not expecting or wanting to meet Lilith or anyone. There were precipitous slopes on all sides to which plants hung precariously. Far away in the distance something glinted strangely—something that in time came to seem the answer to my desires—yet though I noticed it, it did not arouse my curiosity on this uncomfortable day. Intent upon the only thing that did arouse it, I stared at Lilith as coldly, as uncompromisingly as she stared at me. And all the time my temper was rising.

Lilith's gaze fell at last before the intensity of mine. She was shivering a little, I saw, as she said brightly, "I ran away; that is what happened. I ran away as far as I could go. To the Red Sea, if you must know; to the desert."

"Then what did Adam do?" I said. "Did he come after you?"

"*Adam?* Come after *me*? Of course he never did. Being obedient to Jehovah, of course, he called him, and he sent those minions of his: Raphael, Gabriel, Michael, Uriel; each with their sinister little arguments and devious furies. Oh and Sammael of course, since all this happened before his fall. I minded him less than the others, though in some ways he was the most dangerous—having chinks in his own armour, he might have recognised the holes in mine. Could anyone have caught me, it would have been Sammael."

"But he didn't catch you?"

"Why do you think God had to make Adam another wife?"

"But I still don't understand why he had to. You still haven't told me *why* you ran away," I screamed out, for how could she be so stupid as not to know that she must tell me?

At which she enquired to my astonishment, her voice almost as loud as mine, "Tell me this then, Eve. Do you like lying underneath?"

"Underneath what?" I asked, bemusedly. "And what's that got to do with it? I never heard such a stupid question."

But with so many desperate questions I scarcely knew any longer which one I myself was asking. Lilith smiled almost sadly, and cried in an angry voice—at least I thought it was angry—

"Can you really be so innocent, Eve? It's got everything to do with it."

"What? When?" I was insisting.

"At night. Or in the day if you like. You and Adam—when you—I don't know what name you and he use for it."

It was only then I realised what she was talking about. "You mean *fucking*," I asked with relief; almost instantly I realised something else and asked again, this time appalled, "Did you—I mean he—were he and you—he with *you*?"

"Of course," she answered simply. And it was obvious, I don't know why it had not occurred to me before, but it had not. I didn't like it either. I did not know why not. When I pulled Adam's body into my mind's eye and placed it hard against Lilith's body, it did indeed seem a most natural conjuction. But I still did not like it in the least bit.

Meanwhile Lilith was saying meekly, "I'm sorry, Eve, to destroy your illusions." At which I shrugged and threw a stone from the ledge where we were sitting and counted the number of times it bounced against the slope.

"What is wrong," I asked at last, bitterly, "What is wrong with lying underneath?"

"Why not ask Adam that question? He, you may have noticed, doesn't like it either." Then she softened a little in face of my distress, adding more kindly, "Everything is wrong with it. And then again nothing. Except what it stands for. Which is why I just can't do it, why I ran away. It wasn't that we couldn't enjoy ourselves in other positions—but—oh Eve, how I embarrass you by talking to you about such things . . ." she was mocking again now, for it wasn't embarrassment I was feeling at that moment.

She went on watching me, steadily, and at length, to divert her, and because I needed the answer as much as I feared it, I asked, in a low voice, "Do you think he still likes you? Do you think . . . ?"

"Oh, he never liked me much. Not the way that he likes you. He did not bother to make me out for a start—he'd have been as happy had I not been made at all. He did not quite dare tell me and certainly he was too reverent to complain to Jehovah, just the same he often hinted at it. And though I did not see it at the time I think he was right probably to resent me. What need does Adam have of anyone besides himself? He loves God and the garden, he's devoted to his work—in other words he's perfect.''

"He loves *me*. He needs *me*," I cried desperately, scarcely able to bear it.

She looked at me pityingly and said, "A little, maybe. After all you were not made the same way that Adam and I were. It does make some difference."

"But how was I made?" I asked—at which she sighed and laughed, saying, "Oh, Eve, Adam's rib; you mean you don't remember?"

"Not entirely," I said. "How should I? Do you remember how you were made?"

"I might," she replied. "And that might have been the problem. But I can't talk about it now. I suspect, Eve, that you are in no state to hear." And she was right, at that moment I was not fit to learn such truths. All my doubts and fears crowding in upon me, my mind kept returning over and over to but one thing that she had told me; to the image I had of her body and of Adam's.

"Surely when he fucked you, he must have liked you a little?" I pleaded, though dreading her answer, as much as I needed it.

"He lusted after me, there is no doubt of it. Is that what you're wanting to hear?" she asked coldly. And when I remained silent, continued relentlessly, "To judge by the way he was the other night, he still lusts after me a little. Yet the significant question is do I still lust after him? He's a better lover than any demon, that is one thing for sure."

I looked at her more blankly than ever. At this turn of the conversation—yet who but I had turned it?—I felt very cold and sad, at the same time little hot flames were boring away at me, forcing me not only to catch but to pronounce this same prickly word that I had not heard before today; that I would have preferred never to have heard.

"Suppose," I said, "Suppose he were to lust after you more than he lusts after me?"

"Does it matter?" asked Lilith. "Do I have to remind you

again, Eve, of the more significant question? Do I lust after—do I want—*him*; not the other way about."

"But how could you *stop* wanting him?" I wailed. As for me, at that moment, I had never wanted him more.

Lilith sighed. "You'll understand one day, though I doubt if you could now. It isn't a simple thing at all. The fact was that in the end the price of my submission was too high; that other things were more important. At which point I ran away."

"Then what made you come back?" I cried out, very loudly.

"To find you of course, my only sister. It's very lonely in the desert." She spoke in such a way it was clear she meant it. But when she added, mockingly, "Would you rather I had not?"

I answered—I bellowed it. "Yes. No. *Yes.*"

Then at last I burst into tears, got up blindly and ran down the hill away from her, slipping on mosses and lichens. There was a pool of water in the valley into which I hurled myself, the cold shock doing little, however, to dowse the flames lip-lip-lipping away.

"Eve, don't," said Lilith, surfacing beside me, and gazing into my eyes with deep and loving anxiety. "Eve don't. It is no matter."

But I thought it was one. I seized her by the shoulders and kicked out at her with all my strength, and then, the tears again starting to my eyes, waded furiously to the other side of the pool, jumped out, dripping wet, and ran up the stony hill into the arms of Adam. His eyes for Lilith, standing near the little pool below us, he held me for a moment only. When she beckoned him towards her he pushed past regardless, and slowly, reluctantly, walked down the slope towards her.

Chapter Six

When Adam arrived that day in Lilith's stony valley I do not think he'd expected to find me there with her. I think his first—and usual—instinct in the face of both of us was to turn tail and run. On the other hand, dogged as he always was, not to say obstinate, once he had made up his mind to confront her, not even my presence, it seemed, could shift him. Worse, he ignored me— appalled and afraid at the way she seemed to draw him towards her, I half feared for a moment they might fall into each other's arms and perform there in front of me the act I could not bear to contemplate; at least as they performed it.

In fact she did not advance one fraction of a step towards him. He halted at least six feet from her. Then they stood and stared at each other—it must have been more than a minute before at last, like a wind raising itself very slowly, or a fire painfully struggling to life, he began to shout at Lilith and she started shouting back at him.

First he bellowed at her to go back where she had come from. Then she accused him of never having loved her; of having, in his lust, used her no less than he used the rocks from which he wrested his mountains and with much less affection. In his turn he accused her of trying to destroy our marriage as she had once destroyed theirs; of trying to corrupt me, moreover. At which Lilith looked at him mockingly and asked where he had learned such words.

"Aren't you more afraid of her corrupting you, Adam?" she said. "*Aren't* you? But then of course you should be. Because she *may* corrupt you—and if so it will have nothing to do with me."

"Aren't you teaching her to behave as you did? Never to do anything I asked? And why did you never do anything I asked?"

"For much the same reason *you* did not do what *I* asked," she replied. "But as for Eve . . ."

"What about Eve? What does . . ." Adam hesitated for a moment; long enough for Lilith to add very quickly—though he tried to interrupt her he could not manage to do so—"Bones fester, Adam, even in Eden, if taken from their place. And tell me, what happens to the space that's left behind?"

All this was beyond me. I did not understand one word; but neither it seemed did Adam, who accused her of being too clever as usual, and returned to his tirade the more energetically. Never, before or after, did I hear him use so many words. (Had she always drawn them out of him, I wondered? Had that been why he had not liked her? *If* he had not liked her?) And never had I felt more strongly than at this moment how much longer they had been in the garden than I had; how much I didn't yet understand about how things could be between a man and a woman. My lithe young flesh seemed my only defence against their experience, as well as against the wiles and the schemes of everyone around me, not least our father, Jehovah.

At the same time I admired and longed for both my friend and my husband. How magnificent Adam was; how fiery Lilith; how wrong it would be for either to bow down before the other—so I thought in the beginning, wondering too, fearfully, what need they could ever have had of me. But then as things went on I saw how easily she rode him. Aching to see it, each time I watched him charge head down in the wrong direction, missing her allusions, destroying his own arguments, I longed to restrain him. And yet I dared not do so.

And what was the point of it? Even I, ignorant as I was, could see quite clearly after a while that their words went round and round. Perhaps they had always done so. In the end Lilith, still wet from head to foot after her immersion in the pool, was throwing at Adam the same taunts with which she had started, while he could only yell over and over that she had never known what was good for her, and that clearly she never would.

"I'll tell you what's good for me," she replied very quietly. And before my eyes—as if I did not already feel like a child held at bay by the shared past of its parents—she began vivaciously to flaunt herself, thrusting forward her wet hips, her breasts, her thighs in a way I could not comprehend and yet which overwhelmed me with shame and terror. Adam having his back to me, I could not see his expression as he regarded her. I hardly needed to. I saw him shudder. I heard him start groaning.

"Isn't it better to desire me, Adam? I'm still your wife, after all. And afterwards you can go and make mountains as you always did and forget all about me; *I* won't undo you." Her eyes grew hectically bright as she spoke, her looks ever bolder.

"And will you lie underneath," Adam whispered—by now I had crept up behind him; I heard every word he said. "Will *you?*" she whispered back. And when, pitying their foolishness, at the same time as hating them I laid my hand on Adam's shoulder, he gave me one anguished look and turned back again to Lilith.

Who was lying down beside the pool now, her legs wide open, calling. "Am I meek enough now, Adam?" she mocked. At his blundering towards her, she leapt to her feet; caught unaware he stumbled, put out a hand to her—and then—it might just have been an accident—missed her altogether and fell into the pool, surfacing a moment later, his hair and beard streaming. "*Am* I only your servant?" she asked him, with vicious amusement as he stood, abject, in the water. "*Am* I only your whore?" But as I fled back up the hillside torn both by pain and guilty laughter, I heard her whispering behind me, "Do you love me, Adam?" I turned my head at that; when there came no answer, saw her, too, flee away alone up the other side of the valley.

Next moment, to my amazement, she began screaming with wild laughter; she shouted from the hillside above him, "You mean you call this place paradise? You call this place Eden?" Astounded, I resumed my flight. At the head of the valley I glanced back again, but she had disappeared entirely, while Adam, streaming with water, was following me, slowly.

*

That night, for the second and last time in the garden, Adam failed to find me. I wept all night, not knowing the way of things. How could it be like this, I wondered in my quieter moments. Jehovah told us to love each other. We *do* love each other. Though I love Adam because I want to, not because Jehovah says so.

At some point, I remembered how the serpent had once, rather crudely by his standards, tried to find out what I saw in Adam. For his own part he'd made clear that his grudging respect for the landscapes my husband made was outweighed by his scorn for Adam's lack of practical skills on the one hand, and of technical understanding on the other.

"What is the point," he had said, "of his making such things and not knowing how he does, or even what they're made of, let alone how to use them?"

Though cautious about engaging in such arguments in case I ended up damning Adam rather than defending him, I had pointed out that the serpent's friend Sammael was not exactly skilled in such directions either; yet the serpent did not despise Sammael for it.

"Can you imagine despising Sammael?" the serpent replied so fervently I suspected irony; I had been taken aback to discover none. "Besides, as a magician he can override everything."

"So can Adam," I said, remembering Adam's bowers; the way his volcano had erupted from the earth.

"Why do you keep defending him, Eve? He has no wit, he's not amusing company. I suppose the truth is that you like him in bed?" At which I had blushed, because I did; protesting all the more fervently thereafter that Adam was just as clever as the serpent, if in a different way. But as I said these things I had also found myself thinking that I really did believe it. And that I found his cleverness, if not as entertaining as the serpent's, of a kind I understood much better. That I felt more comfortable with Adam than with anyone else in the garden, because he seemed part of me, as I seemed part of him.

I had not dared at the time to express this to the serpent—it would have made him much too angry. As it made Lilith angry when, less wary of her in those more innocent days, I'd tried to tell her about it. "What do you expect my dear—you *are* part of him," she had said mockingly, upon my declaring that I felt part of Adam. Though hurt by her tone, I had not wondered about the meaning of her words. But I did now in the loneliness of the night. As I wondered, weeping, if Adam would come back to me, and how I would live without him; indeed if Lilith would, and how, if she did not show her face again, I would live without my sister. At which thought I wailed louder than ever, shutting my eyes so tightly I did not see daylight come or Adam come either, though I heard him weeping when he did; felt the sobs shaking his body as he enfolded me.

And from then on, surprisingly, things went on much as they had always done, as if that one quarrel had cleared the air—or most of it. This was still Eden after all. Though no longer as trusting, I could learn to live with jealousy, or so it seemed; not least when I had seen the way things were between Lilith and my husband. It is true that I still did not care to imagine the conjugal embrace of Adam and my sister; yet I refused to let myself dwell upon such things. Similarly they seemed to go out of their way to avoid one another. (It was only at my suggestion, after all, that Lilith had encountered Adam in the first place, it occurred to me; no doubt it was mischievous of her to have taken me up on it.) And though both searched my face sometimes for signs of their ex-wife or husband, this rarely led to quarrels between us; not many quarrels anyway—if in the company of either Lilith or Adam it seemed my fate from this time on to feel a vague disloyalty to the other, I was beginning to accept that feelings could not always be simple.

Yet Adam at least never mentioned anything that had happened; indeed he avoided Lilith's name altogether, though questioning me closely sometimes, more anxious than angry, as to what I had been doing with myself.

As for Lilith—I noticed that she had started to sneeze again, quite violently sometimes. And I was alarmed once or twice to hear her say things like "When I leave the garden". I would assume she was teasing; at the same time I'd be overcome by a terror at the prospect of losing her not much less powerful than the longing I also felt sometimes to live alone once more with Adam, as I had done in the beginning.

So at last we reach my longings—so many of them these days they seemed to consume my energy, to be everything that I lived for. Perhaps I should list here all the things for which I found myself longing.

To begin with I longed to be alone with Adam, and to talk freely with him—for him to talk to me without the shadow of Lilith between us.

Contrariwise I longed for Lilith to stay in the garden.

I had also begun to long to reach the sea or ocean. That was the name, I had discovered, of the strange glint I had seen in the distance the day I met Lilith up the mountain. Adam, when I asked him, claimed that he had made it. But it was Lilith who had led me up another hill, pointed out the distant gleaming, and said, "That's it. You had better be careful. After all, that was where I ran to." But I had hardly heard what she was saying, in my instant desire to reach it. So pure and clean and simple, so close to the sky, it seemed to hold the answer to every confusion, quite why I did not know.

Another longing I had of course was this: to tell stories like the serpent. Yet as frequently as he demonstrated this art to me these days, when I begged him to show me how to do it, he shrugged and said I did not know what I was asking. What, for a start, did I have to tell stories about? he demanded. A question I could not answer, remembering the lively events with which his stories were filled, while I knew of no doings other than my own. Nonetheless I assumed that if he would only show me how, my head would soon ring with all kinds of dramatic happenings, and that in due course, given a little help and practice, I'd find myself constructing verbal artefacts no less polished than those I was learning to produce using his other arts. (Just now, for instance, he was showing me how to glaze my clay vessels before I baked them in the fire, with pine resin and other such substances.)

*

And finally there was this desire; the most pervasive of all of them. The apples of the tree of life having ripened at last, there was no place in the garden where I could escape them, their scent followed me everywhere I went.

In some ways, of course, my desire to taste the apples did seem the simplest of my yearnings; Adam and I were allowed to eat this fruit. Yet I could not eat unless my husband ate with me, and because of the troubles we had suffered we had still not managed to mention, let alone discuss the matter. I supposed it was because the apple tree stood close to the other, the forbidden tree; and from that Adam shrank with such horror—the more horror, it seemed, after his confrontation with Lilith—I did not like to remind him it was there.

How absurd of us, I decided one morning; and determined to visit the apples to view their condition—it would be foolish, I thought, to wait until they were rotten. Setting out, however, I met the archangel Raphael and at once started with unexpected, unnecessary guilt.

"Is there anything you want, that you long for especially, Raphael?" I asked him, hastily, my mind running on all that I desired. He looked puzzled at first and then faintly disapproving.

"If I *have* a want," he replied, stiffly, "if I have a want it is only to worship God." But he did not speak with the icy fury of Michael or with Gabriel's cold fire or Uriel's burning frigidity. He spoke sincerely, his tone between piety and apology, his gaze far away.

"You angels are so predictable, Raphael," I said. "It was a real question. I hoped you could be helpful."

"No more predictable than you, Eve; if you're reflecting as I suppose on the matter of the forbidden fruit."

"The apples are not forbidden," I reminded him. "It's just a matter of deciding when to eat them."

"Wanting them might be forbidden," said Raphael. "Had you thought of that? At the very least it might be dangerous."

"Dangerous to whom?"

"To yourselves, of course. To us," he chided me.

"Dangerous to the angels? How could it be? What harm can we do you now?"

"Nevertheless," said Raphael apologetically, "you give rise to some local uneasiness. The spheres are, as you know, so very finely balanced; big ones within little ones, so on and so forth."

"Sammael," I said, "is always talking about the spheres. But I never know entirely what he means."

"Don't you?" Raphael gave me a sly, rather careful look.

"And besides," I cried, confused now, for reasons I didn't understand, yet catching from somewhere a waft of the apple scent, which didn't tantalise so much as terrify me with longing, "what is wrong with wanting the apples?"

"If it is," he replied soberly, "the apples that you want."

"What else?" I demanded desperately.

"What else?" he asked, wringing his hands together, "Don't tell me you do not know." If an angel could be said to look at once fearful and agitated, Raphael did at that moment; his fear not like yours or mine or Adam's, however, but much thinner and purer, like air at the top of a mountain. It contained too, for all its genuine concern, an element of simple calculation—Raphael's feelings always did; he was not only the most sincere but also the most mathematical of angels.

At once, having set the awkward thought in my head, he left me and I continued on my way. When I reached the trees, the river was running so low I did not need to swim. I waded across— though snuffing up greedily the scent of the apples I did not have eyes for them any longer, only for the other fruit, the one I did not desire with its new, faint tinge of purple.

I had not noticed till then, I think, quite how differently it grew from the other. Apples sprang from the stems which had first borne flowers, amid leaves springing from the same stem. The figs, on the other hand, swelling independently out of the branches of their tree, were little snouty things, like growths, having no grace at all as the apples did, only a crude, almost animal vigour. Indeed they were animal, I thought, repelled at once, as also by the leaves, which reminded me that day of deformed giant hands, like a mockery of my hands or Adam's or the serpent's. The very wood and bark of the fig tree was much smoother than that of the gnarled apple tree, the very smoothness was sinister; it made the fruit still more untoward, unnatural looking, as if the tree was suffering from some disease, not fruiting in the normal fashion.

I had never looked at creation in such a way before. A moment later confused, almost ashamed of having done so, I gazed at the fig tree more respectfully, finding its vigour and oddity interesting, even exciting, rather than deformed and dangerous as I had a moment ago. And then I found myself wondering again just exactly what knowledge was and why it should deserve that ailment called death—no one in the serpent's stories had been given one for pursuing the other. At the same time I wondered why we should have been given the tree of life. I knew what life was, I had it, and I knew it went on for ever, what else *could* life do? So what need did I have of that fruit? Why did it smell so delicious? Why did I long for it? I ignored the faint mocking echo I heard from far away—was it Raphael's voice, did solemn Raphael know how to mock?

"Holy, holy, holy," came the angelic echo; fading almost at once to something more like "Hollow, hollow, hollow. Hollow. Hollow. Hollow."

"I'm alive," I defied the echo. "Nothing can harm me. Not even you, Raphael; or Gabriel or Uriel or Michael." And at that I reached up and picked a fig from the tree. I felt its stalk snap neatly, and held its suspicious green, its dull grooves, in my hand, pressing them very lightly with my fingers, at which the flesh gave beneath them, a little more certainly than before. For good measure I picked a leaf too, pleased by its smooth round stalk. And then, with a whoop of amazed, proud, reckless mischief I cried out aloud, "So much for you, Raphael," and flung down both fruit and leaf, thinking as I did so how much my more frugal friend Lilith would disapprove of such wasteful behaviour. ("You can't afford to waste anything in the places where I live," I'd often heard her say, but never realised how soon I, too, would be obliged to take note of such baffling, uncomfortable notions.)

Chapter Seven

Was it at that moment, after I had thrown the fig away, yet still sensed its grooves upon my palm, that the possibility occurred to me of telling Adam and Lilith's tale? If so I did not like it—for not only could I tell their story, they could tell mine, I realised; or the serpent could. Very soon, maybe even simultaneously, I determined that my storyteller must be—had to be—was going to be—myself.

Yet what, after all, was there to tell about myself? How much more exciting or interesting to tell stories that had nothing to do with me; stories, for instance, like the one the serpent told a few days later about three virtuous men called Shadrach, Meshak and Abednego, who had been cast into a furnace even hotter than the furnace in which he smelted his metals, because they insisted on worshipping Jehovah, instead of gods made of metal and stone. Fortunately for them they owned enough magic of their own to cool the flames and to walk about among them, saying prayers meanwhile to their stone and metal gods and mocking the less material one who had tried to burn them to ashes.

"Where did you learn such strange things?" I asked him. "Who are these men? Jehovah only made Adam, so who made *them*? Where do they live? When did they do such things?"

"But they have not done them yet," said the serpent, mysteriously.

"Then how do you know?" I asked in bewilderment.

"I know everything," he teased me, shifting and coiling his body all the while. I did not trust him for a moment. Nor did I understand one word of what he went on to tell me—something about Eden being outside time, I think. I understand better now, having been so long outside time myself, having surveyed sadly all the foolish things that he described and many far far worse. Yet he didn't always describe them correctly. Maybe he did not know as much as he claimed to. Maybe, mostly, he was guessing. Maybe he lied deliberately and told them the way he wanted me to hear, or the way that he wanted them to be.

One thing I had noticed was that the mysterious word "children"—or more often "son" or "daughter" came up again and again. All, as far as I could make out, were younger and for a while smaller versions of the father or the mother, constructed by them in some way I was unable to fathom, since the serpent never mentioned that parents of both gender were needed in the act. Yet the idea you could have and love and care for a younger, smaller version of yourself had begun to appeal to me very much. I felt I shared the anguish of the man in one story the serpent told me, ordered to kill and eat his son because he was starving. Indeed the man could not have been more delighted than I was when God produced a sheep in the nick of time, so that after all he did not have to slaughter and devour the boy. (To me, though, in those days, it seemed no less strange to eat a sheep than it was to eat a man. Had I, I wondered, got the story wrong?)

Perhaps, it was because of such stories that I gave birth to a new longing at this time—one I could hardly be aware of; Adam and I being complete and perfect, there was no question that we could reproduce ourselves in Eden. Just the same, I would stare after any cow and her calf, any cat and her kitten, any sheep and her lamb, with a strange kind of envy, for all that I was unable to recognise it as such, let alone imagine, yet, that we might engender young of our own. And I observed in loving awe the cat I once found lying beneath a thicket, purring and purring, while one by one there emerged from the hole at the back of her body—with what wonder and terror I saw it widen and open— little wet, ratlike creatures, which she licked and attended; which snuggled up against her, blind as they were and started nuzzling at her belly.

I wept for joy afterwards; and did not know quite why I wept, unable to identify my longing. Nor did Lilith explain it when I told her what I had seen, though she looked both sad and sardonic and said, giving a little shrug, "One day, Eve, you may understand the things I have taught you." At which she'd departed abruptly as if I had annoyed her.

And when I told Adam he merely grunted, much too involved at that moment in some creation of his own. "It happens all the time. What of it?" he complained. As for the serpent . . . I did not for some reason mention it to the serpent, merely begged him the harder to teach me to tell stories, that being one longing I could identify.

He wasn't standing in my way, he said at once, to my surprise; he even ordered me to tell him a story if I could. But no matter how long I looked into my head I found nothing there, apart from Lilith's tale which I didn't think was any of his business; and apart from pallid versions of tales I'd learned from him. It didn't stop me trying to relate one of them, though I didn't get very far. I don't know which silenced me more effectively, his boredom or my consciousness of its pallor, almost as soon as I'd started declaiming it.

"There you are," the serpent said at last, "precisely. You can't tell stories till you've something to tell. How often, Eve, have I told you that?"

"Too often," I replied gloomily. "Which means it's time I went to look for some stories of my own." Yet I didn't know where or how to begin.

"Do not blame me," the serpent was saying soberly, "if you don't care for the endings you arrive at." I thought he meant by this to warn me that I risked being drowned or burned to ashes, yet chose not to know it; or rather, more accurately, was not capable of knowing it, despite the shivers of what was it?—dread—elation—excitement—that began running up and down my back.

If half the problem in finding a story is to recognise a story when you have it, I did not know it then. When within a short time of setting out to look for one, I met an immovable stone barrier—in other words the wall of the garden—I assumed it had been put there to thwart me; that the adventures all lay on the other side, and that to reach them I would have to circumnavigate it by one means or another, none of them obvious. Four times my height, the wall stretched as far as I could see.

It had not annoyed, merely puzzled me last time I had encountered it, in Lilith's company, just one among many new things I encountered in the garden daily; and all of them, I assumed, created for my delight. How strange, I thought, remembering such bliss; remembering too how benign the wall had seemed in comparison with the way it seemed today. The sun no longer upon it, the stones were colourless and cold, fitting together so closely they gave no foothold to any living thing. There was barely a trace of moss or lichen, let alone creepers up which I might have climbed, and thereafter seen to the other side. No grass, even, grew within its shadow.

Any idea I had that it was part of Adam's creation soon faded as I gazed at it; the fitting and dressing of the stone, the neat coping laid along the top had been made by hands not minds, hands much more skilful than his. The serpent's hands perhaps? Or Lilith's, I wondered—it was she who had pointed it out to me, yet if she possessed such skills she had never bothered to warn me. Was everyone plotting against me, I asked myself wildly, at this point, beating my fists against the wall. Because I had begun to feel that something was being plotted, though I did not know why or what. If not, why were there so many mysteries in the garden? And why did Jehovah not speak to me these days? Ever since he'd raised his storm, he'd not visited me except in the company of Lilith or Adam and then kept all his conversation for them.

In a while, weary of such thoughts, I began walking along the wall, hoping to discover some gap, or to come across a tree maybe, growing close enough to let me see beyond, assuming I could climb it. There had been a tree once on the other side, a tree with leaves like hands—the fig tree had leaves like hands too, I thought. If only it were here; or any tree. Today it was not apples or figs I was after, just friendly branches. Yet there wasn't a single tree in sight.

For hours that day, I walked without respite. I don't know exactly at what point the wolf first joined me. He did not make his presence known, and locked in my maddened and melancholy thoughts I never looked for him. It was only when—inadvertently I think, the wolf the one animal who'd never showed us any affection—his flank touched my leg, that I looked down and noticed him. Then, mutually, gratefully, each of us acknowledged the company of the one other creature in the garden who'd not only discovered the wall, but was prepared to pad interminably round it, in the hope of reaching what lay hidden on the other side.

The wolf made no obvious response to my greeting. He did not even look at me; I barely caught a glimpse of his unfathomable grey eyes, let alone saw myself reflected in them. Though there was no sun and we walked at an easy pace, he was panting, his tongue lolling out across his sharp teeth and speckled gums. Perhaps he had already been running for a long time. If so, it had not left him hungry; when I picked some berries from a bush and attempted to share them with him, he shook himself and plodded on regardless, head down, tongue out, while I ate, disconsolate, not simply because the berries tasted sour.

We walked until evening and nothing changed at all. Whichever direction it turned, whichever way the sun, the wall still kept on throwing its shadow over us. Towards the end of the day I was ready to give up seeking stories from it; but not to give up seeking stories, if I had to go on all night. At this point, as if I realised that I need not stay with the wall unless I chose to, my spirits lifted a little. I looked down at the wolf, and he, to my surprise, for the first time looked up at me. He only waited a moment after that. Having folded his tongue back into his mouth and closed it, he gave me one glance that seemed to be forgiving my weakness and another that said he expected I'd be back. Then his body gathered up its power and launched itself—I watched his long lope till he was out of sight. Never once did he ease his desperate pace; never once did he look behind him or move more than inches from the wall.

Alone, however, my desperation eased considerably; I even

began to enjoy myself a little. Taking the opposite direction from the one that I could have expected to lead me to my husband, I set out into country I had never seen before, looking for nothing that I knew for certain.

While there had been no trees in the vicinity of the wall, where I came now there were if anything too many of them for comfort. They did not make a wood, quite. Sturdy trees, evergreens most of them, they were close enough, however, to bring back the sense of imprisonment that I'd lost when I'd left the wall. The sun going down threw their shadows across my path like bars— traversing each one boldly I would not let myself be contained. Could I make a story out of all this I wondered? If I did, it would scarcely be exciting. There were so many characters in the serpent's stories; myself and a silent wolf did not seem enough to people mine. Besides what events—let alone dramas—were to be found here in the garden? Was it possible, I demanded aloud—not that anyone answered—to snatch stories from Paradise, from the Garden of Eden?

With a shiver that was equally pleasure and alarm, I flung my arms out then, and summoned anything or anyone. For the moment, nothing and no one came, not even an animal. Where were, I asked myself, all the insects and birds and animals—there were none to be heard or felt or seen; I had never before encountered such isolation. Maybe my loneliness could make a story; if so how to wrest excitement from this inbred, inactive, melancholy affair?

I did not stay alone for long. It is true that as things were I could have imagined almost anything. Darkness falling fast, I could not but doubt that life was everywhere, where there had been no life before. Not life that I knew, however—not friendly animal life—this was the life of things which shouldn't have been alive. The very trees seemed to be marching alongside me. I had never been afraid of trees before, except when animated by Jehovah's rage; but Jehovah, I knew, did not bring these to life, these trees, unmistakably, animated themselves. Or if they did not I animated them. Indeed there seemed no limit, suddenly, to the number of ways in which I could look at and shape my surroundings, though till recently I had assumed that there was no more than one.

I even understood at last what it meant to be afraid of the dark. Unlike my husband, Adam, however, it wasn't the dark itself I was afraid of; what I feared was what the darkness contained.

Which was no doubt the reason Sammael chose that moment to confront me with his barren magic. But then Sammael, angel and magician—so the serpent would have it—always did pick his moments very carefully. In that way, as Jehovah's arch enemy and at the same time most fanatical votary, he strove with his whole might to oppose Jehovah's will (and so to fulfil it possibly; but who am I to say?).

And yet there was no Sammael in the beginning. In the light of rising moon, all I saw was a tree; a tree moreover that I had noticed earlier, before the sun had set. Of course I'd mistaken my first angel, Michael, for a tree at first. But his tree had been ordinary, one pear tree among many, whereas I had never seen another tree like Sammael's; even in broad daylight I'd viewed it with apprehensive awe.

An evergreen, it had appeared both more squat and more generous than the usual evergreens, the angular firs or pines. Its clusters of needles were softer than theirs, and much closer set; its branches spread very widely, its trunk was split, making a cave at its heart. It looked besides a particularly dark and bitter tree, with its near black needles, its red berries so bright amid its darkness they seemed to give off their own light.

I had still been hungry then. I'd gathered one of the berries and broken it open, sniffing suspiciously at its yellow seeds and acrid juice before casting it down in disgust. Afterwards I'd ceased to be hungry. Now the moonlight had bleached out the colour of the berries, but since at the same time it intensified both the tree's bitter smell and its outstretched, commanding darkness, I could not mistake it, any more than I intended to let it deter me. In a moment, gathering up my courage, I stepped out once more, giving it a wide berth.

Though the branches reached out so far, so unavoidably, that the needles brushed my skin, I had actually managed, my heart beating very loudly, to take a stride beyond them, and had even begun to take another, right foot firmly before left, when something brought me to an abrupt halt. Still, helpless as I was, my striding feet as if rooted to the earth, I fought to keep my eyes facing straight in front of me. Yet the struggle was in vain. The tree—or whatever it was—maybe it wasn't a tree any longer— was much too powerful to resist. After a bitter struggle I was forced to turn my head and as soon as I had done so, that was the end of it. I could not have removed my gaze, even if I'd wanted to.

But I did not want to. The tree, more than tree, had cast a spell on me, the way it kept shifting and swaying, shrinking and swelling very restlessly, very strangely, though there was no wind to blow it. Its ghostly branches writhed and twisted themselves first into one shape and then another. Meanwhile the moonlight turned its berries into little white sparks which came and went, relentlessly, ornamenting the darkness like fishes swimming in a river. They could not possibly, ever, have been red.

"Sammael?" I asked, "Sammael?" The question was quite beside the point. For all this arboreal guise I knew Sammael as well as he did himself. Which is not to say that he didn't wholly bewilder me—watching my ever growing shadow spread itself masterfully across the moonlit space where his would have been yet was not. I wondered, not for the first time, why the angels had no shadows.

I was of course mortally afraid of him; to be anything else would have been extremely foolish, and I was much less foolish than I had used to be. At the same time, my shadow continuing to grow, I felt wickedly exhilarated, and even glad for once that the serpent was elsewhere. I felt that Sammael and I were conspiring in some way, over what I did not know. Nor did it seem to matter very much; in fact I could not have cared less.

Deliberately I took my eyes away from him. Just as deliberately I put them back, to find the tree again, then Sammael, then tree, all in rapid succession; then Sammael and only Sammael. If I hadn't known better I would have thought he played tricks to amuse rather than frighten me.

Not that he looked at me still or spoke to me, or that I spoke to him; that kind of acknowledgement could wait for another meeting. Instead without words, without signs, we made visions of the garden. At the time I could not tell whether they belonged to him or me, whose head provided them and showed them to the other's; I knew only that they kept on coming, whether I wanted them or not.

Once, I saw Adam and Lilith wander hand-in-hand, a vision which made me cry out in huge pain. Later I watched Jehovah walk alone, interminably, in the endlessly pulsating yet endlessly empty garden, surveying the fruit that stood rotting on every tree—no matter how he raged the pitiless light continued shimmering all round him, opening and shutting each day, each night, as regularly and pointlessly as a blind man blinks his eye.

Again I cried out—but the pain was different this time, and different again when instead of Adam and Lilith and Jehovah, I saw myself in the garden, trapped and surrounded, my fears taunting me from behind each growing tree. At once I began to whirl about in anger and anguish, delivering blows at everything within reach. Not one blow fell—but it might have done—between myself and Sammael, it was hard to say which of us was angrier. If I pitied him sometimes, no doubt I'd have done better pitying myself. The way he laughed at me I daresay he knew it. I hated him above all; as he hated me.

I do not think it was hate, however, which brought him at the last to one story the serpent hadn't told me; assuming it was Sammael who brought me; the enmity between my first-born sons was still not a story told in words, and it could have been that I brought myself. Indubitably, it became at once my story, though naturally I did not understand that yet or recognise that the grief I felt at its unfolding was the special grief of a mother for her sons.

★

At which Sammael departed as silently as he'd come, and I continued on my way, the faintest of bitter smells still lingering in my nostrils. In my utter bewilderment I knew this and nothing else; that where the darkness before had been quite empty, now it was full of everything that ought to have been familiar. I found myself surrounded by animals—yet their eyes luminous, their teeth and claws gleaming in the moonlight, they didn't seem like the friends that I met during the day. Not one of them spoke a language that I knew; until now, I'd understood everything they said. And though all of them had shadows, though they kept me company the whole night long, at dawn, when I came to where Adam lay asleep, they melted away as if they feared us, but so silently, I only realised they had gone because of the very young, lion-coloured kitten, left behind by its mother, which suddenly began mewling at my feet.

I picked it up after a while, pitying its distress, wondering if it could be one of those I had watched being born. With an unfamiliar but pleasant sense of tenderness I held it to my breast, rubbing my chin against its head, enjoying the warmth and softness of its fur, the buzzing of its purrs against my naked skin; until in the strengthening light the narrowed pupils of its golden eyes turned it into a creature less comfortable to know, a creature which delicately unsheathed its claws, and drew them as delicately across my left nipple.

A moment later it bit the right one. It was only curious, I think, it did not mean to wound me. Indeed it did not wound me—just startled me so badly, I put it down with a small cry. At once, giving a birdlike chirrup, it ran off to where its mother waited at the edge of the dark wood, leaving me with a sense that I had lost something, I did not know what.

I remembered the kitten again later that same day; after I'd told the serpent about the wolf and the wall and reached the story that Sammael had given me—the one I might, just, have given to myself—the tale of the two warring brothers. A woman's body had opened as if it was a cave, I told him, awed all over again at the thought; had expelled first a red-haired son, later a fair-haired son. (Why hadn't he told me, I asked in passing, that a woman had so much to do with the advent of sons? At which briskly, even uncomfortably, he ordered me to get on with my story.) The red-haired man had grown as big as Adam; so had the fair-haired man; the elder planted gardens, the younger tended flocks, and both loved one woman, their sister, the way that Lilith and I loved one man.

I came to a halt then; as far as I was concerned this was the end of the story—indeed the unfamiliar smell of blood having no power yet to frighten me, I assumed that everyone lived happily in the end, unlike in all the serpent's stories. I was taken aback when he demanded impatiently to know how my tale ended. It had ended, I said; one of the brothers had kissed their sister, that was the only ending. If I learned another I would tell him, of course.

"Is that a promise, Eve?" he asked, smiling with suspicious kindness.

"It's a promise," I told him, smiling in my turn; but I found myself uneasy suddenly. When he went on smiling I told myself, doubtfully, not to be so stupid.

So that was the first story I ever told. One part of my own story, had I but known. Maybe even then, as I told it, long before I guessed this was my story, I suspected that the dazzling entertainments the serpent went in for were not the kind of stories I was going to be able to tell. He constructed his both effortlessly and neatly the way he constructed all his other artefacts; whereas I would have to dig mine as slowly and painfully out of the depths of me as Adam created his mountains or as he himself dug metals from the rock.

Chapter Eight

After what I had witnessed between Lilith and Adam, my first meetings with my sister had not been easy. By now, though, slowly, almost without realising it, we'd regained some of the trust that we had lost; not quite the same heedless wholehearted trust, perhaps, in my case, but in some respects a wiser one, helping me to understand how much more Lilith and I still shared than just rivalry for the affection of my husband. Indeed it was astonishing how soon, from our main bone of contention, he became our mutual problem, his vagaries something we could share and always had shared, if we'd but known it. Until gradually my jealousy, the origin—or so I believed—of my confusions, appeared a pale, if diseased shadow against the other feelings I was learning.

(Which is not to say it did not still lie in wait and pounce when I least expected; as did her jealousy, even fiercer than mine, I came to realise, finding fuel everywhere, not just in its first source: Adam.)

You could even say that what I learned during these intimate discussions was not only of use to me throughout my marriage, in Eden and out of it, it also brought Lilith and me closer than ever before. Yet there was a melancholy edge to this closeness, a sense of pending loss all the more poignant for my growth of understanding.

It helped perhaps that the confrontation between Adam and Lilith had made it quite clear to me how unsuited they had been. Having observed also, too closely for comfort, the deadly attraction between them, I never quite lost my fear that they might meet secretly. Yet it was not a fear I took very seriously, except when Lilith chose to exacerbate it for reasons for her own. At such times, I would regard the fact that Adam these days avoided us entirely, that the three of us were never in the same company, as sinister rather than healthy. For a day or two again I would rage and wish Lilith far away, my mind turning over and over all the questions she had not yet answered, merely hinted at, concerning her beginnings and mine.

It did not make matters any easier that my meetings with her these days were so rarely unobserved. If Adam stayed away from them, Jehovah did not; I felt his presence much more often than was comfortable, scrutinising each growth in our mutual understanding, encouraging and deriding us by turns—spying on us was how I put it sometimes, observing with equal alarm his anger and his satisfaction.

Though he never appeared to speak a word, at least not to me, Lilith's sudden distraction used to make me realise that he had things to say to her, serious things, I could see, though they spoke beneath their mental breaths. From Lilith's expression—the very intensity of her frown—the abruptness of her gestures—I might sometimes guess the nature of their exchange; negotiation, it could be; alternatively discussion. In each case I was afraid for her, for being so brisk and businesslike; for being so consistently immovable. At the same time I was more afraid for myself, caught by every wind, it seemed, because I had to be.

At other times, in place of himself, God sent his angels to watch over us. All four archangels, Gabriel, Michael, Uriel, Raphael, interrupted us on one occasion or another—if they too addressed themselves mainly to Lilith, I could and did understand every word they said. Each asked sternly, I remember, the question to which she had still given me no satisfactory answer, that is what she was doing in the garden. Yet they did not seem to expect an answer; nor did they get one, except for the same one she had given me—that she had come looking for the comfort of her sister. Now I think that for all her mocking tone, it was the proper answer, and that I ought to have trusted it; that I should have asked rather why Jehovah had let her come.

But I did not trust it—I pushed her over and over, till, her voice exasperated, her laugh very brittle she cried one morning, "I thought the serpent told you everything these days; I thought he'd passed on to you all the famous stories." (The barbed way she put this reminded me that Lilith's chief jealousy these days concerned the serpent not Adam. As well it might, given what he had taught me.)

"Not all of them," I said. "It seems there are quite a few left to learn. In some cases I know the beginnings—in others I suspect the ends. In yet others I don't know the beginning or the end." At this point I hesitated and looked at her questioningly, wondering if I should tell her the story I had learned from Sammael. In the end I just said, a little cheekily, "I don't know the beginning or the end of my own story, let alone of yours. I don't know how you were made, for instance, or even how I was. Differently you said; but how could it be so different? You said you would tell when I was fit for it. Am I not fit, by now?"

She looked at me wryly then. "Oh very fit. But are you ready to hear it? Let alone ready for the effects of such knowledge." At which she sneezed three times, as if it was a warning. And when I said nothing, went on, much more lightly, "You do know such a lot of other things, these days, young Eve. Aren't they enough for you?"

"I do not know as many as you," I replied gravely, certain of it.

"Be glad of that while it lasts then. No, don't look so be-wildered. It isn't the end of the world to be ignorant."

"Then what is?" I asked, a curious and delicate question for one as ignorant—or innocent—as me; at once I knew it, going so far as to wonder out loud what I had meant.

"I'll tell you," was her answer to this, after a long pause. "I'll tell you all of it, if you will tell *me* Eve, what happened to you the day you found my wall."

"How do you know I did?" I asked, in astonishment.

"As you have just this moment pointed out, Eve, I know a lot of things; not least that you were bound to encounter that wall on your own one day; not least how secretive you've become recently; how much there is that you do not tell me." ·

(And it was true that for all our closeness, I did keep many things to myself, these days, particularly when they arose from my friendship with the serpent.)

Very quickly I agreed to Lilith's terms, on the condition that she spoke first; a condition with which she did not quarrel. She simply led me out of the dark wood in which we usually wandered at this time, the brisk pungency of its pine trees more pleasing to our mood than the languorous scents of the meadows, squatted down, scraped up a handful of the dry red earth, spat on it over and over till it was soaked right through, and then began moulding it this way and that between her fingers, the same way that I moulded clay to make the pots in which I arranged the fruit for our supper. The end of her labours, however, was no bowl or dish. Instead she held out to me a manikin of sorts—though it had a head like a man or a woman, two arms and two legs on which to stand upright, it took me a moment or two to see just what it was.

"Well," she said. "Well? and *now* what do you think?"

I looked in bewilderment from her creation to her and back again, the bizarre thought which came into my mind denied immediately by the crudity of the manikin compared to the subtlety, not to say delicacy of Lilith's features.

"If you mean what I think you mean," I said at last, laughing at her, "Jehovah must be a great deal better at such things than you are."

But Lilith did not laugh. And gradually because it was so, because I had no option but to believe, she made me believe it, that Jehovah had moulded both Adam and Lilith from the red earth itself—in that way she gave me the only image of him that my mind has ever managed to hold to. Jehovah was no longer a voice, he was two huge, manipulating hands smeared with, dripping with, earth, like my own hands when I moulded my pots, the lines on the palms and fingertips etched out in red.

"And now," she said, "you see why I couldn't lie under Adam."

But I could not quite see it at the time. As it was only much later, during my loneliness in the desert before Cain was born, that I understood what she meant when she went on to say a little wistfully, "My solitude you see, Eve, my independence, is both my heaven and my hell."

"But why should it be so different for me and Adam?" I asked, remembering what I had seen of her and my husband together. "It's not like that between us," I added wistfully. "It is really not like that."

"Listen to you, Eve," Lilith jeered, pulling herself out of melancholy. Throwing her manikin down so hard that it split into little pieces, she added, more viciously than ever, "That sounds just like my little Eve. Longing to be back to back with her husband, front to front, front to back, back to front—thinking his thoughts, laughing his laughs, following his every order."

These days, however, I did not let Lilith get away with such things. "You know perfectly well," I said, "that this is not what I want; this is not how things are."

"Then how are they?" she asked cunningly, hunching herself up.

"You know how they are. I've told you."

"Just as you know how you were made, Eve."

"Show me," I ordered, "as you showed me the other." But of course she could not show me—though she demonstrated on our bodies the place on Adam's from which I had been taken, and in that way made clear to me there had really been a wound, the one I kept imagining so vaguely but so fondly.

I felt awe then. Also disinclination just for the moment to explore the implications of this sweet, disturbing fact, that I was truly part of Adam, and that he was part of me. Reminded—both by the awe I felt and the similarities I saw between them—of what I'd seen in Sammael's story, I proceeded instead to fulfil my part of the bargain, telling Lilith as briefly and as simply as I could, of the vision I had been given.

"Can you imagine," I ended, "can you imagine so absurd a thing as a woman guarding a man in her belly then drawing him out from between her legs? Have you heard of anything so stupid?" Choosing still to ignore any likeness I saw in it with the way that I'd been born, I was laughing all the while; felt the more surprised, therefore, at her brisk and stern response.

"Don't you ever listen to a word I say? Certainly I can imagine it—it's the most natural thing in the world. How else do you think the cow got her calf or the cat her kitten?"

"A man," I said, indignantly, "is not a kitten or a calf."

"Isn't he? In some kind? Do you of all people doubt it?"

"Do you despise men then, like Sammael?"

"Why should you despise a man, let alone a woman, to liken him to a kitten or a calf? Now you sound like Sammael; or Adam for that matter."

"And would *you* want," I asked, "to take a man from your body like that? And who put him in there in the first place?"

She gazed at me then, the tears springing to her eyes—the tears sprung to mine too, for no reason I could see except that, moved and longing and sad for both of us, I was beset suddenly by some vague, unhappy memory of her talking once about giving birth to demons. I felt angry too, with Sammael and the serpent, with Adam, the angels, all the creatures who would not, could not understand these things. (Though Adam ought to have done, I realised; from whose body I had been taken; who had been wounded on my account. At which thought, in fear and terror, I acknowledged for the first time, in the marring of his perfection, my power over him.)

"And who put *me* into Adam's body?" I asked next, clinging to my childishness for comfort.

"As if you didn't know," she said. "And as if you didn't begin to understand his purposes. And as if you aren't capable now of using all your knowledge."

"Can't you use it too, Lilith?"

"No," she bellowed at me. "No, I can't, you silly little bitch."

Her pain terrified me, not least because I couldn't share it. Yet as it eased, so did my terror, not least because it was I who helped ease her pain at that moment. I forgot my wariness. Putting my arm round her shoulder I murmured that I loved her, and how brave I thought she was, how strong, the kind of stupid things I'd say to my daughters in the years to come. And for once, to my surprise, she did not push me away; she laid her head upon my shoulder and told me I was generous and kind and that she wished I could have stayed the same, that we could stay together always. I did not like the sound of that. All the same we grew a little happy; we could have stayed that way a while, I think, had we been allowed to remain alone. But we were never allowed to stay alone these days. Shortly we wandered into an orange grove to find ourselves overwhelmed by the sweet pungency of oranges on the one hand, the violence of voices on the other; Sammael and the serpent arguing as usual.

Chapter Nine

Yet nothing else was as usual in the scene that Lilith and I came across, apart from the fact that Sammael and the serpent were arguing. For today Sammael's voice came from the air, he was riding on the serpent's shoulders, an extraordinary sight, making them both appear more powerful than ever. How strong the serpent was, for instance, to bear such a burden; and how arrogantly Sammael rode him, using his hands ostentatiously, both to emphasise his point and to demonstrate an undoubtedly impressive ability to keep his balance without their help.

Moreover they exchanged their arguments about the advantages of one tree over another, that is of life over knowledge, that is of the apple over the fig, while standing by a stone cistern full of water, which reflected the orange tree leaning over it, reflected each little orange floating there, reflected the serpent bowed by the weight of Sammael—but did not reflect Sammael at all. If you looked no further than the water you'd think the serpent was arguing with himself. And when Sammael shuddered at the sight of me and Lilith, though the water reflected his shudder it did so only in the body of the unwilling serpent, who tried in vain to steady both of them.

"Sammael has no shadow as well as no reflection," I heard myself saying loudly. But they all, even Lilith, hushed me; though they did not hush such statements as "Knowledge is power," proclaimed by the serpent; or "Nothing is more powerful than the prospect of eternal life" (Sammael of course); or the question; "What's knowledge worth in death and pain?" Sammael again, his voice cruelly sarcastic. The serpent winced quite openly at this. If in his turn he needled Sammael slyly, even cheerfully—"What's good about eternity if you spend it fall-ing?"—his eyes remained yellowish, opaque and full of pain, while the air around us grew colder and colder. Lilith was shivering, I noticed; very soon so was I. Yet there was not one mention of what seemed to me significant, and might certainly have had some bearing on the problem; the delectable scent of the apples; the more cautious, at the same time more voluptuous, maturing of the fig.

I stopped listening after a while, until, in due course, they joined forces and pushed the argument our way—something about the pliability—and lack of pliability—of female gender, I gathered; meaning that whatever the female did she couldn't get it right.

"I'm not pliable," I could not help whispering then, wonder-ing why Lilith left me to answer them. "I shall do what I need to. If it means I have to eat those vile figs." Hardly daring to take in what I'd said, I clutched Lilith's arm, and leaned across the cistern—upon Sammael's shying from my reflection, the ser-pent's abruptly vanished. In their place both Lilith's and my reflections stood in the water; such cold water now, icy even, growing icier by the second; I could not melt the ice any more than I could put out the fire in the oranges that floated amid the ice. The scales on the serpent's arms, I noticed, glittered as if dusted with frost.

Gazing numbly at our reflection, I saw rather than felt at first what Lilith had began to do; the way, provocatively, she first touched then began to stroke my breast. Her mouth was open a little; her tongue was tasting her lips—

"Tell me about death," I shouted at steed and rider, reminded by her voluptuous hand of the one great mystery that remained.

"Sooner," she hissed viciously, "sooner ask them to tell you about birth. As if they could."

But now, disregarding the serpent's appalled look, I'd laid my hand too on her full breast—to calm and comfort her?—to reassure myself?—to mock the serpent as she was mocking him? (But should I want to mock the serpent?) I could see both hands and breasts in the water; as if in response to our warmth it had begun to burn instead of freeze. The ice melting, the snow stars faded from the oranges, and they started to breathe out the spicy scents that the cold had forbidden for a while, though, till I smelled them, I did not realise it had. Indeed only Sammael and the serpent remained still frozen, the one, majestically riding the other, who as majestically carried him. Meanwhile their voices expelled single, icy little words, forming huge, meaningless, snow-covered statements, which melted at once in the heat of our reflections.

Lilith had suddenly begun laughing hysterically—she could no longer keep her hand steady on my breast. Soon she took it away and tried to cover her mouth to hold back her spluttering, before crying, for the second time, "You mean you call this place, Eden? You call it paradise?"

At which her laughter grew so uncontrollable I had to lead her away from the stone cistern; not till I took my last look at the way its stones were laid and dressed did I reflect that the serpent must have built it. Away I marched, meanwhile, from steed and rider, Sammael and the serpent, feeling like a reluctant but loving mother leading a reluctant but loving daughter and stopping her mouth and drying her tears of laughter.

"Do you want me to stay with you, this evening?" I asked Lilith at last, when she had calmed down a little. Though no longer afraid I was taken aback by the brisk way in which she answered,

"Oh no. How can I? Not now, after I've seen how you've changed. There's so little time left, don't you see?"

Immediately she went away, leaving me alone with those last three dreary words. Because I did see, all too well; had clear in my mind I would lose her, and in far too short a while.

As it proved; for it was only the day after that I heard Lilith sneezing before I saw her. It did not occur to me till then that yesterday she had not sneezed once—now, on the other hand, she did not seem able to stop. Eyes streaming, nose scarlet, she was choking herself into a large leaf, from a sycamore tree I think it may have been, though she stood underneath an ash.

She was irritable, naturally. I made the mistake when she had recovered herself a little—I could not but make it, everything with Lilith appeared so urgent now—of asking why she had not sneezed at all yesterday; and, still more dangerously, why she had not defended herself, let alone me, against the insulting innuendoes of the serpent and Sammael. She did not answer the first question; instead regarded me with something that looked almost like a sneer. As to the second question—she reflected a little and then replied, angrily, "What's the point? They only say what they say to irk us. Alternatively their minds are immutably made up. You might as well argue with Jehovah."

"I do sometimes," I said. "Argue with Jehovah."

"More fool you," she said. "And anyway, you only think you do."

"What do you talk about with Jehovah then?" She stared at me again. I repeated, panic-stricken, suddenly, and even to my fury jealous. "Just what *do* you talk about? About the fact he allows you back into the garden? Why *does* he allow you in the garden?"

"Is that any of your business?" she asked, rather coldly.

"If it has to do with me it is," I said.

"And what makes you think that it has anything to do with you? That you are so interesting and important?"

"Then what else makes him talk to you for so long?" I replied, not to be daunted.

"Does it never occur to you, Eve, how much easier it is for him to talk to me? I'm an old acquaintance; he's tried and failed to change me, he knows where he is. Whereas you . . . how can he be comfortable with you? You *can* change, and he knows it, he, after all, conceived what has to be. Which does not mean to say that he wants it."

"He talks to Adam," I said helplessly, having no wish to reflect on this extraordinary, not to say painful notion; that not even Jehovah always knew what he wanted.

"Adam is easy. He's contented with the garden. He's good company when Jehovah needs it. Whereas you . . ."

"Company?" I interrupted her. "What do you mean *company*. Surely Jehovah can't be *lonely*."

"Can't he?" she replied coldly. Leaving me to be assailed suddenly by an unwilling, unhappy memory of the vision I'd had from Sammael. Again I saw Jehovah wandering in an empty and overgrown garden, all the fruits rotting on the trees—was that to be the end of everything? Then how could I bear the guilt of inflicting it upon him, assuming it was me that was going to? And how could *God*, this justice—breathing, fire-love-wrath-breathing, force, power, mystery, whatever you chose to call it, be lonely, when he had all those angels at his beck and call? Was that why he'd made us? To keep him company in the garden? If so, appalled among other things at the intimacy of such a glimpse, I had no desire to know it.

"What else does he want?" I pleaded.

"What do you think he wants?" Her tone turned dangerously mild; in a moment she'd been overtaken again by further paroxysms of sneezes.

"What does he want of me, for instance?" This answer, suddenly, was something I needed very badly. Lilith seemed the only person in the garden not likely to palm me off with the "Blessed be he, let's praise him," kind, of which the angels were so fond. It did not stop her offering me such an answer; the sardonic glance that went along with it was overtaken instantly, however, by yet another sneeze.

"Eve, Eve—what does Jehovah ever want but praise?" she said.

"But praise does not seem to be the only thing he wants from *me*," I replied—here, though, I took her hand—"He tells me not to eat the figs for instance, and the angels are always telling me my obedience is praise. I'm quite happy to praise him in that way, all I want to do is forget the wretched fruit. Yet I'm never allowed to. If he's not asking me questions about them, the angels are. And if he doesn't want us to eat, why does he put that tree right by the other one, the apple tree, and make the apples smell so marvellous it's hard to forget them day or night?"

At which, speaking my confusion aloud for the first time I grew more terrified than ever. If Jehovah did not know what he wanted; if he too could be lonely—what certainty was there?

Where was it all going to end? And did I really want it to end in the place towards which I seemed, inexorably, to be heading?

Lilith meanwhile, her colour still high, her eyes bright, glittering, even a little feverish, stood swinging my hand gently and at last said, to herself virtually, like the last whisper before winter of an almost leafless tree, "So you've noticed have you? I told you you were listening to too many of the serpent's stories."

"What's the serpent got to do with it? Can't I work anything out for myself?" I replied, my indignation helping to calm me.

"That's the whole trouble, Eve; you're ready to work everything out for yourself, now, in one way or another, and arrive at your own conclusions. You've grown up in other words. So what use am I to you, or Adam for that matter? Neither of us can change in Eden. We are equals; we are just as we are."

"Adam isn't any longer," I said. "You know he isn't. He lost his rib." Saying which I knew—or began to know—for I was not able to accept quite yet the loneliness of such a conclusion—that this was the nature of my power over both of them, Lilith as well as Adam. Not least because I recognised, as Lilith could never do, that Adam's weakness could also be his strength; and that he would most likely follow wherever I chose to go.

Lilith spoke almost viciously now. "Why are you looking at me like that, Eve? Like a greedy cat. Like a sad bird considering its prey."

"Your nose is running, Lilith. There's a drop hanging from the end of it."

I spoke as roughly as she did; as if I too was breaking the threads in the web that bound us with the crude blade of my crude words, with the still cruder edge of my voice.

And so it seemed over between us—and so it was—yet all was hanging in the balance still. Nothing was possible except what was going to happen; yet nothing was decided till the moment that it did—not till the moment Lilith ran shrieking from my life—not till the moment I sank my teeth into the fig.

At some point in that long day it began to rain, a fine mist shrouding everything and setting a network of drops on Lilith's hair; and at some point after this—the rain had still not eased I think—she seized my arm and we began to dance. I don't know why we danced; I only know we did, wheeling and cavorting, our hair, mine red, hers black, each with its net of water drops, swinging out around us. I also know how madly we danced in the end, obliterating all our sense and our surroundings. We were beside ourselves and inside each other; we were trees and clouds and grasses, driven by winds of our own making—how we exulted in them, nothing existed besides us, wild women that we were. Frail as our wet bodies felt in each other's arms, our love had turned to such frenzy we could have rent all the other creatures of the garden, animals, angels, Adam—even rent what passed as Jehovah, that crude old man, than whom we seemed so much older and mightier—rent them with our sharp white teeth, our furious claws and afterwards devoured them till they lived only in our bellies, in our heads, in our ever increasing, ever more delightful madness.

I don't know precisely when Adam came; or why he did, though I do know how greatly he feared us. The rain had stopped by the time I noticed him, and for once he stood his ground, our frenzy reflected in his eyes, his hands tight with fear, the sweat running down the hairs on his chest. For one moment I was angrier, more dangerous than ever, my anger almost entirely for him. At the next it had faded, I'd lost all desire to rend Adam or anyone. And only a little after I found myself, separated from Lilith, whirling nearer and nearer the place where he was standing. I danced for him now, there was no doubt of it—to my further surprise I noticed Lilith, sulkily, begin to follow suit. In the end we were both dancing for him, gloomily and politely, Adam meanwhile devouring our bodies with his eyes. Though I noticed they held to Lilith's body longer than they held to mine—was it in desire or horror?—both, I think, most likely—my twinge of jealousy was replaced almost at once by a sharper twinge of grief, because it did not matter any longer. (At which point did I only imagine hearing Jehovah, with or without his angels, etherially, laugh?)

★

No, Lilith never said to Adam, "Take your wife, take her. She's all yours, Jehovah help us." For a time I invented such a story, but it was not so. As I've said everything was decided, and yet not decided, and we had plenty of reasons already but absolutely no excuses. My belonging to Adam—as he belonged to me—had nothing to do with it.

You need excuses for action as well as reasons; without them the most inexorable of fates will keep on hanging in the balance. But even an excuse is useless unless you choose as Lilith did to take it. Indeed in the end she not only seized her excuse, she made a drama out of it, an over-inflated one, if you ask me; despite the death it spelled, the one I still weep for.

It was true I had a hand in it. As it was true she gave me the strawberries, not the sweet wild ones I'd preferred in the beginning, the bigger, juicier kind that the serpent used to cultivate. All I did in some more thoughtless than malicious moment was pick out the largest of them and offer it not to her but to Adam. At once, seeing the pain on Lilith's face, I knew what I had done.

"Lilith," I pleaded—"Lilith"—as Adam, voluptuously almost, devoured it—"*Lilith*." Too late, she had picked up a handful of the berries and crammed them against her mouth—maybe some went in—most made an ugly crust about it which moved with her lips.

"We can pick some more strawberries, Lilith," I pleaded; "I only gave him one. It doesn't matter."

"Doesn't it?" She moved her crusted lips ever more slowly and painfully. I wanted to scream at her, without knowing exactly what I objected to, as she added, "They don't grow, strawberries, in the places where you're sending me to live."

For a moment I could not believe it, she patted me so lightly on the cheek. But she kissed Adam much less lightly, turned her back on us, or on the angels who had suddenly appeared from nowhere, then started to walk away very slowly.

I began to believe everything then—I had to. She had not gone twenty yards before, giving sneeze on sneeze, she started to run, not forty before she let out an eerie wail that split my heart in two and still does if I remember it. I felt myself turn pale and cold, in a moment was shivering uncontrollably while I watched her scuttle off, wailing like an owl into the distance, without hope or fear or love, leaving every word she had spoken still hanging in the air. It was as if the mist gave way before her, there was no mist where Lilith ran, her shoulders heaving with sneezes I could no longer hear; for ever and ever and ever it seemed I watched her out of sight. My first loss, it was also my first death, I swear it, for all there was no broken body. I felt in some ways to blame, moreover, in this case as the other.

PART THREE

WOMAN

Chapter One

Thus, having described my first loss, I reach the last part of my story; not, in the beginning, the easiest of times. I am still unwilling to describe my emotions as I wandered alone after Lilith's departure, weeping, reliving our life together over and over. I reproached myself sometimes; if I had done this; if I hadn't done that, all quite besides the point, as I was already well aware.

The serpent meantime left me severely alone; which I now think was more likely to have been clever than kind of him. (He would certainly have preferred me to think of him as clever.) I conclude, in particular, that he would have found my desolation embarrassing at such close quarters; certainly he did not come near me till it had eased to a cleaner, more gentle sadness, and even then approached warily, as if I might bite at any minute.

"Would you like me to tell you a story?" he asked one day, giving me a sideways look. He'd never asked if I would like a story before, simply embarked on it. Still, now, my indifferent nod was enough encouragement. He gave me a man slain by an angel—before he'd time to explain how the man was resurrected, I protested that I wanted to hear about women for a change, about mothers and daughters. At this he obliged me, not very obligingly, with one woman eaten up by dogs, and another who'd cut off her husband's hair, though to no possible advantage that I was able to discover. At least it made a change from the tales with which I was subsequently regaled, about lost babies in baskets or patriotic giants bullied by little upstart shepherds, or trumpets that blew down walls (I wanted one of those I murmured, gloomily), or wise men who knew the language of animals. I knew the language of animals, I protested at this point—what was so very special about that?

Nothing would deter the serpent. His stories fizzed through my head like shooting stars, giving me no time to note them before they faded. He must have realised he no longer dazzled me. Once he asked, slyly, if I was still looking for my own stories; when I muttered not, it seemed, not at the moment— indeed I felt I had as many as I wanted, even if I didn't know their ending—he laughed, very loudly, screwing up his face to such curious effect, all his scales looked lopsided. Which goaded me at last into telling him I did not want to hear any more of his stories either.

He looked put out at first, then replied equably enough that it didn't matter very much, he'd told me most of the ones he had to tell. Soon he went away, the dismayed hunch to his shoulders making me want to run after and embrace him for my sake and for his; but for his sake and mine it was impossible to do it.

A little while later the ants' nest revealed itself to me. It was the winged queens I noticed first; they had made the mistake on their wedding flight of seeking love upon my body, crawling all over my belly and sides. I felt quite affectionate in the beginning, and can hardly tell you at what point I began to find their swollen abdomens unpleasant, began, frantically, to brush them from my skin.

Which was not the end of it as I'd expected. For when I looked about me, I saw pouring from a hole in the dry earth a host of other insects, a myriad of little winged ants struggling to fly amid further myriads of black ants and amber-coloured ants and fat blind grubs.

Was this ruthless prodigality to be the end of all my knowing? I wondered, my sense recoiling in fascinated horror. If it was, I wanted no more of it. I wanted only to wander in the garden as I had done in the beginning, thinking of, knowing, absolutely nothing.

Too much knowing had lost me Lilith, I decided, going off to meet Adam; I should be careful to do nothing that might lose me my husband. Thus I greeted him more enthusiastically than my grief had let me greet him recently, and did not let myself feel hurt because he held me rather warily at arm's length as he often did these days. I could not blame him for being wary, knowing what I knew; remembering the savage stranger I'd become in my dance with Lilith, a stranger of whom he had good reason to be terrified. When on the other evenings he had tried rather clumsily to placate me, it had been all I could do not to burst out crying, wondering if we would ever feel easy with each other again.

Tonight, just the same, I did my best to quell my doubts; I stroked, loved, reassured him. And before long to my surprised delight he was reassured—I almost wanted to warn him against being so trusting, at the same time as I wanted to weep for joy. In that way, sooner rather than later, more quickly than slowly, Eden once more wove its tentacles around us and locked us to its embrace. I imagined, a little sadly, Lilith telling me what a fool I was. But in my head I answered her pertly enough—isn't it better this way? Is there anything wrong with loving Adam? For what did it matter if in some respects neither of us could make head or tail of one another, provided we were happy? I'd learned at last that happiness was something to be valued.

It is true that our marriage in the fullest sense could not begin until Adam and I ate the fruit; perhaps not even till that moment he came back to soothe my pains, then laid his head upon my breast alongside my new-born son. And yet at this time, children as we were, it was as if we had found some well-protected spot, some place in our beginning, where we could be as comfortable together as we became right at the end of Adam's life, when he was an old man and I an old woman; when, cleansed for the most part of inconvenient desires, we waited calmly for an end to which we'd long resigned ourselves and now almost wished for, and meantime grew as close as the two ancient olive trees in one of our courtyards, their roots and branches entwined so inextricably we could not tell where one began and the other ended.

★

Those last glorious days in which we wandered Eden together seem so few now, looking back. At the time they seemed infinite—even then, in some way, I knew that they were not.

I dared question Adam at last about everything we saw; for he no longer seemed to mind my questions—perhaps because most concerned his own creation. Had he really made *this*? I'd ask innocently, then answer myself—no, not possibly, I could not believe it, I'd say—I was goading him, of course. And sure enough, before long, and with a smile on his face, he would raise a hand and cause whatever it was to vanish, tree or bush or stream or hill. Immediately, he'd make them spring up again, sometimes alongside a new hill or stream or tree or bush he'd created before my eyes, giving me small and intimate glimpses of his art that before he would not have dared to.

His making seemed to have ceased to cause him pain. This Adam wasn't white-faced and silent before he set to work, nor did he droop with exhaustion afterwards. This Adam, smiling, conjured marvellous things out of nothing and made it look easy.

One day, for instance, he created a tree, such an extraordinary tree there cannot have been another like it in Eden. Indeed it was a whole Eden in itself, containing all life and every one of the seasons. New green leaves mingled with mature green leaves and also with autumnal ones—crimson and yellow, brown and orange. Among them were buds and blossom and falling petals, while sour green fruit hung next to ripening yellow and ripe red berries of the most succulent kind on which we gorged ourselves, alongside all the other creatures the tree harboured and nurtured: squirrels, for instance, birds, beetles, caterpillars, butterflies. Every colour, every shimmer of wing or fur or hide, unsuspected one minute, would vibrate the next before our delighted eyes. Our ears meanwhile were filled with animal and insect voices, greeting us as carelessly and gladly as they greeted their fellows.

"How prodigal you are," I murmured to my husband. "Almost as prodigal as mighty Jehovah."

"Of course," he replied, "I know." His hasty, "Blessed be his

name," added only as an afterthought, we caught each other's eye
and smiled a little; for once, I am certain, we were smiling at the
same joke.

I could have stayed in the shade of the tree for ever. But Adam
that morning seemed unable to keep himself in check—we'd
hardly time to enjoy the tree's bounty before he made a lake for it
to stand by, and caused an island to rise in the middle of the lake's
clear waters. On the island, bordered by white sand, stood a
mixed grove of palm, magnolia and orange trees, the magnolias
rosy with blossom, the orange trees laden with fruit. Even from
here I seemed to catch their scent—whatever it reminded me of
could not at that moment make me wary. There was, immediately, nowhere else in Eden where I so longed to be.

"As soon as you reach one place, you want to be in another,"
Adam complained mildly. "Can't it wait until tomorrow?"

"Why did you make it, then?" I asked, over my shoulder.
Taking a running dive I plunged into the water, and avoiding the
narrow reeds that grew at its edge, swam strongly for the middle
of the lake. I assumed the splashes I heard meant my husband was
following. What I had forgotten—if I ever knew—was that
Adam could not swim.

The fact he'd only made this lake to please me made it all the
worse to see him thrashing about so helplessly, his hair and beard
draped with weeds. My uncomfortable memory of last time I'd
seen him in the water was most likely the reason I spent the next
few hours attempting, with difficulty, to give him the elements
of my skill. I don't know which surprised me more, his persist-
ence or my patience, nor which of us was most pleased when he
managed to swim several strokes. Perhaps not till then, through
the affection with which I watched my husband struggle, did it
occur to me how much for granted I'd always taken him, except
when seeing him through the eyes of Lilith.

Meanwhile the island grew more alluring by the minute. I
could hear hidden birds calling from inside it; as for the trees, the
prickly vigour of the palm eclipsed neither the orange trees' dense
foliage and brilliant fruit nor the more delicate dignity of the
magnolia blossoms. The sight of the three species standing in

such precise harmony set me to wondering why Lilith, Adam and I could not have managed to do the same.

That night we two, husband and wife, attained the pinnacle of our bliss, in or out of each other's connubial embrace. The island's abundance almost equalled our wedding feast; besides the fruits there was even wine to drink. I don't know where it came from, it was much too sweet and heady to be of my making, but when I asked Adam he replied simply, "I made this island for you, Eve, and imagined all joys on it," thus silencing my doubts. Like everything else—the dulcet breeze, the fragrance of the trees, the soft calling of the doves—I had to accept it as a gift.

So I did accept it; though it was, undoubtedly, a merrier gift than most. As the darkness fell and the small night creatures— hedgehogs, for instance, and bushbabies, with their babies on their backs—came out to greet us, we lay against a magnolia tree, Adam's arm around my shoulders, laughing helplessly with the world and with each other. Until at last, while I watched him, he lumbered to his feet and began dancing to some tuneless humming of his own which defied any attempts of mine to add to it. The sight of his clumsiness irritated me a little; at the same time, perplexingly, it filled me with such tenderness and love it stopped up the breath in my mouth.

A fat yellow moon squatted on the horizon now, throwing shadows of the trees across the clearing, among which Adam's shadow lurched and weaved. Though beginning to grunt with the effort, he continued doggedly bending and turning, swaying sometimes from side to side, meanwhile humming louder all the time, more and more tunelessly—if the rhythm he gave voice to and the rhythm of his movement did not coincide exactly, they counterpointed each other in a way that began to make me feel dizzy. Or maybe what made me dizzy was the wine we had drunk from its strange and transparent container, like water, but solid, revealing the liquid it held inside itself.

No doubt it was also the wine that made Adam lurch about so wildly. Several times he collided with one tree or another, clinging to their trunks, gasping, before going on his way. Several times, the way he swayed almost to the ground, it seemed he'd never regain his balance; but on each occasion, somehow, he heaved himself upright and went on in ever decreasing and slower circles, of which I, I began to realise, alarmed, was the centre. At last, having no further to go, he stood right over me, reared up like a bear, as broad-shouldered, almost as hairy in the cool, uncaring, honey-coloured light.

He was grunting now rather than humming. "Eve, Eve," I made out. "Eve, *Eve*." I'm not sure if he said, "I love you." If so it was the first and only time. Then he fell down at my side, reached a hand across my breast, sighed, groaned and fell asleep. The whole night long he lay, snoring gigantically. Meanwhile I watched the moon rise and fall again leaving the stars to glitter more brightly and wondered why they, like my head, seemed to keep on flying in spirals.

Next morning, alas, inevitably I suppose, we wakened out of bliss, our heads sore, our tempers uncertain. Adam did not seem able to bring himself to look at me—too conscious of my dishevelment, it never occurred to me he might be shamed by the memory of his dance. As we grumbled our way back across the lake I wished that the heady scents of the island had not been replaced this morning by the still headier scent of the apples; stronger than ever, it followed us wherever we went. Neither of us referred to it. Adam had never done so, while I, for the moment, was nauseated rather than tempted.

Chapter Two

But the scent of the apples did not go away. It stayed with me thereafter, the fruit hanging heavier and heavier on the tree. And within a day or two, my nausea gone, my longing for it returned, more intense than ever, bringing all my other and now seemingly desperate longings. Every hill I climbed, it seemed, I would find the river and the island and the trees of life and death lying below me; in the distance, always, stood the glinting of the sea.

Though I did not yet dare speak of the apples to him, Adam sensed my mood certainly. He began to go away again most mornings, and reappear in the evenings looking tired, as if, aware that not much time was left, he had spent the whole day engaged in frantic creation.

The serpent, on the other hand, seemed to have as much time as I needed. I would beg him to tell me once more the stories I had spurned, wondering meantime about the story I had told him. I had even begun to suspect that the serpent spoke the truth, that the story of the woman and her rival sons did indeed lack its ending; but where I should find it I did not know, nor why it should concern me.

I asked Jehovah once, but he who'd called himself my loving father seemed indifferent to the question. Though he had taken to visiting me again these days, he seemed removed from us, compared to how he used to be; no matter what I demanded he granted me only the half of it, if he granted anything at all, as though, already committed to our departure, he preferred to gather up his solitary strength. At times I almost wished he would mock me as of old, or show his arbitrary yet reassuringly mighty wrath in which I could forget myself in exhilaration or terror. Our recent bliss now seemed so far away that except for some odd, insouciant, always unexpected moments, I did not feel able for an instant to lose myself, my restless mind, or any of my longing.

One morning I could bear it no longer. "Adam, how much longer must we wait before we taste the apples?" I asked him boldly.

Very slowly and carefully he removed the arm he had only that moment put round me. Holding it out, he inspected it for a minute. Then, just as carefully, he inspected me, his gaze as blank and strange as I had seen it.

"Adam, we are allowed to eat those apples," I insisted, faintly; gathering up my courage I added, "I'm very hungry. Why don't we eat one now?"

"Because, Eve, because . . ." but that was all he said. Afterwards he shrugged and raised both hands in a despairing but humorous gesture, got to his feet and left me without another word.

"Why don't you eat an apple yourself?" he threw back over his shoulder as he went, so light-heartedly, it could not exactly be said that we had quarrelled. A few nights later when he came to find me and I had not yet gathered any fruit, he remarked—again he might have been joking—"I suppose you're too busy hankering after those apples; really I can't think why you don't eat one without me." Teasing or not, he annoyed me.

"Why not if you say so?" I replied tartly, knowing full well by now that I was going to have to eat the fruit alone, but finding it hard to accept, not least because I could not know for certain that Adam would follow wherever I went; but that was a risk I was going to have to take.

The next day I set off determined to eat as I had promised; or alternatively to reach the sea he always pretended not to see, or even to find the end of my unfinished story, the one only Sammael, it seemed, could give me. I did not go looking for the rebel angel—if I tried to find Sammael, I knew I never would. Yet having set my mind to other matters, soon, to my mild surprise, I encountered him, under an olive tree, he at one side of his chessboard and I at the other, a little back from where his opponent would have sat, if he'd had an opponent. For there was no sign of the serpent today. In this game of chess, Sammael's elegant white hands moving both black figures and white ones, he appeared, instead, to be playing against himself.

I don't know how long it took me to admit the truth; about as long probably as it took me to recognise it in the first place; all morning maybe—perhaps most of the afternoon. There were times when I could have been persuaded that Sammael's opponent was myself. If Sammael made my moves for me, what of it? He would have to wouldn't he? No one had taught me the rules of this game. Power take princedom—check, I'd hear echoing in my head—or princedom take seraphim—either way the hand reached out, a black figure was shifted or removed, or alternately a white one—on whose behalf I could not tell.

Upon this thought, precisely, I gave up at last and acknowledged out loud and to myself the nature of Sammael's opponent; his only match; more than his equal; the other half of himself. Yet I don't know, looking back, which of them I feared more, Jehovah or Sammael; which split my bliss into the minutest pieces; which I pitied most deeply.

Nothing I felt availed me however; nothing could avail me against that furious light and darkness shifting from one end of Eden to the other and into the remotest corners of a universe too vast for me to imagine, yet at the same time contained in the movement of the black and white figures across Sammael's chequered board. The battles between Sammael and the serpent had been nothing compared to this; as the sputter of a tiny candle to the blaze of a desert sun; or a shadow of one leaf on the tree that sheltered us to the dark of a starless night.

I cannot tell you whether black or white was winning; I think maybe white was; if so I forestalled it. With what dreadful effort I tipped the board over at last, sent the remaining figures flying; with what fear and relief and love I both felt Sammael's frustration and heard Jehovah's sigh.

★

Afterwards I went away and lit a huge fire. Adam and I quarrelled over it as I knew we would. This time we exchanged definitely angry, not teasing words until he turned his back on me and made a bower so thick and impenetrable not a ray of moonlight could make its way through its walls. Not that I minded—I took to such a shelter as gladly that night as I noticed Adam warm himself for a while at my disrespectful fire.

We did not speak a word in the morning, though we'd hugged each other most of the night. When Adam left me without a word, I assumed his disapproval; still trembling from the day before, I might, however, have misread his mood. I did not entirely understand my own, thus waited till the sun was high in the sky before setting out again in quest of one of my longings— which as yet I scarcely knew, or cared.

I went to the river first, to see the apples. Though all Eden these days seemed to sing a mellow song of late summer blooming, without effort or hurry, I found the river running so fast and furiously that I could not cross it. There must, I knew, have been a storm up in the hills where the water rose; the serpent had often explained these things to me. Yet on such a peaceful morning no storm seemed possible nor could I accept it. Time and again I flung myself into the stream; time and again the currents drove me back, while beyond, the fruit I could not reach mocked at my failure. The apples were rosy; the purple of the figs took on a voluptuous glow. All my longing to eat arriving in full force I sat down at last on the bank opposite the trees and wept from frustration and fury.

In due course I resigned myself, and having dried my tears, set out to find the sea. From the first ridge I climbed it seemed less distant than it had seemed before, making me hope that the walk might be easy. I did not realise how many other ridges lay between us, let alone the steep valleys I would find myself traversing, their thickets and tangles, murmurous with flies, doing their best to prevent me. By the end of the day all that kept me going was the tantalising glimpses the sea offered from every hilltop; the setting sun laid such a path across the water I could imagine myself walking along it and up into the sky.

It was dusk by the time I left the thorns behind and emerged on to an open ridge. The wind smelled strange here yet familiar, I could not think why or how. When I wetted my finger and held it to the wind, I discovered it blew from ahead of me, from the country I'd never seen. But I was too weary to seek any further, too weary even to look for food. Having grubbed up some grasses and bracken, I made myself a bed on the bare slope, lay down and fell asleep before I'd time to regret my husband, let alone greet the constellations overhead. Even so when I started awake a little later, the first thing I noticed was that they had all been blotted out.

I sat up cautiously; before long I was certain—that it was he, that he stayed very near me. Sammael was not a tree this time; nor anything like an angel; more like some solid, immovable darkness that might never have worn wings. Of his usual form only his hands remained; glimmering faintly in the starlight denied by the rest of him, even they were lifeless, as if carved out of stone. All the same, drawn deep into his darkness, into his valleys and caverns, his chthonic visions playing hectically round me, I was grateful to be reminded that there was still a surface to the world, on which light shifted, across which the winds were battling.

In such ways at last, weeping, I reached the heart of my story. Though I had yet to learn how to tell it. Though still, even after Sammael had spoken, I would not—in the garden, I think, could not—acknowledge it as mine. Here are the words in which crudely, roughly, I was to recount to the serpent next morning, from the beginning this time to the end, the vision I had had; that Sammael gave me.

"Once," I said, "once there were two brothers who grew up hating each other; one was thin and angry, the other bluff and broad and more cunning than he seemed. This was the younger brother; he was a herdsman like his father; he had flocks of sheep and cows and goats, and didn't come home very often because he was so busy herding them. The elder brother, taking his skills from his mother, was a farmer and gardener, making gardens and orchards and fields of barley and wheat; he worked hard all day and hardly ever left the homestead because that was where he grew his crops. So it didn't matter too much for a while that the brothers didn't like each other, because they never had to meet, to the relief of their mother, who feared that their quarrel would bring them to some harm.

"But one day, when they were no longer young, too old you'd think to fall in love, the elder brother fell in love with one of his sisters. And immediately the younger one also fell in love with her. Then the anger between the two began to grow more dangerous than it had ever been. They kept giving their sister so many presents she didn't know what to do with them. Nor did either let his brother out of his sight, in case if he did, his rival might persuade the girl to love him. The farmer's fields were neglected meanwhile, so were the herdsman's flocks, until one day some sheep ran wild in the elder brother's ripe corn. Maybe the younger had let them loose deliberately—the farmer certainly thought he had. In his anger he picked up a bone from one of the herdsman's sheep and brought it down on the herdsman's head; brought it down over and over; until his brother fell to the ground, lay twitching for a while and never got up again."

I fell silent at this point, overcome by the memory of the visions that Sammael had sent me—the bloodied bone rising and falling; the face of the one contorted with anger, the surprise on the face of the other—the horror which replaced the surprise as he dived into unconsciousness, at the last his open, staring eyes. Above all there were the appalling blows—sometimes they seemed to fall on my flesh too, sometimes it even seemed as if I was giving them, swept by such furious anger of my own. At each one I had shuddered and jerked; just as the elder brother did, just as his victim the younger.

(And yet again, I'm afraid, the serpent told it wrong in his version of events. "Cain, have you seen your brother Abel?"—it was not Jehovah who put that inevitable and in this case innocent question; it was I, the anxious mother. As it was to me that Cain, desperately weary, reeking of sweat, his hair so dark with dirt you could not see that it was red, made his despairing, un-answerable reply. "Am I my brother's keeper?")

In the end I gathered up my voice and went on very calmly, "Well that was what happened between the two brothers. But after a week or so their mother started to miss her younger son, and to question the elder about him, who just replied angrily that he was not his brother's keeper. Then he too went away, and she never saw either of her sons any more, alive, though she did find the younger's broken body and buried it, with the help of her husband. That is how death first arrived in the world; and that is the end of my story."

Or so I said, weeping again. Though it was not quite the end, as the serpent obviously knew. He looked at me for a while with innocent expectancy and at last when I did not speak, enquired, even more innocently, if I had nothing more to tell him.

"Like what?" I asked, suspiciously.

"Didn't he for instance, tell you the mother's name."

"How did you know?" I hissed despairingly. "But he was lying. I told him he was lying."

And it was true that I had dared contradict Sammael's unspeak-able, monstrous assertion, the only time he spoke to me directly. For this was not a vision like everything else that evening, this he gave me in the simplest of words, pronounced in a way I could not fail to understand by a voice so creaky and rusty he can't have been accustomed to using it, at least not for my kind of speech.

"They are your sons, Eve," he told me. "Your sons, no one else's."

And I had shouted into the air that he lied; although I know now and suspected then it was the only plain truth he ever spoke. He did not need to answer my accusations, certainly. He vanished, taking his darkness, leaving me gasping and writhing. And at once, looking up, I saw that dawn was coming. Above my sleeping place, at the top of the ridge, the trees did not look like any trees I'd seen before; they were weathered and bent and leaned in towards me, away from the country behind. I do not know what I expected—maybe it was the unfamiliar odour in the wind that drew me—all the same I ran up the slope towards them, not letting myself be hindered by the aches of my previous day's walking. And when I reached the top of the hill there it was, at last, reaching as far as I could see, all my heart could have wanted; the sea itself, glowing in the light of the dawn with a strange dull pearly light that heaved and moved in no way I'd seen light heave and move before, just as the voice of Jehovah spoke to me for the last time while I gazed at it as to an equal, in a way that meant he loved as much as feared me. And I felt about me, also for the last time, the gentle, ruthless, earthstained hands of my father and my mother that had enfolded me at my birth and again on my wedding day.

Between me and the sea the wall ran relentlessly across yellow hill and plain and valley. A familiar figure was skulking in its shadow—though he raised his head and sniffed the air in my direction before padding out of sight, I do not know if the wolf saw me. I bowed to my fate almost immediately, and after acknowledging the sea I turned my back on it and the wolf and the wall and Jehovah, went back to my husband, to the island, to the trees of life and death; that is to the fig and the apple and my intolerable decision. For by then, as the serpent was unkindly to point out—the nearest he came to asking what it was I really wanted—I did not know which I dreaded most; that Sammael had told the truth; or that he had been lying.

Much later, towards sunset, I found Adam under a cedar tree looking cheerful and easy. But when, overjoyed to see him, I flung myself into his arms and begged his pardon for staying away so long, he only looked bemused, appearing not to have noticed that we had spent the night apart.

Such blind insouciance may or may not have been the reason that on this penultimate evening in Eden, my grief for Lilith renewed itself with almost its early fury. Even Adam noticed my sadness after a while and asked what was wrong. But I did not want to tell him. Though he tried to comfort me at first, he grew angry eventually. "You've got me, haven't you?" he shouted. "You're in Eden. What reason do you have to weep?"

Unable to explain what else I was afraid of, what Sammael had told me, I was exasperated enough to tell him that I was missing Lilith. And when he protested, reminded him calmly that he, Adam, had needed Lilith once.

"That's different," said Adam. "I needed her as my wife."

"Well, I need her as my sister."

"I don't see why. What good did she ever do you? You were contented with things as they were before she came."

"You mean," I replied, quietly, "that I never tried to persuade you to eat the apples?"

"Why does everything, always, have to come back to that?" answered Adam, morosely, looking away from me.

The sun low on the horizon now, the light around us was warm and comfortable. Adam's skin glowed in it, his hair took fire. Neither he nor the garden, its generous, mild blooming full of murmuring insects and contented birds, had ever seemed more desirable than they did at that moment. I especially loved the bird that started hopping at our feet, greeting us with a sweet hoop-hoeing sound, the crest on its head upright, golden, and almost as vigorous as the bright eyes it turned busily between Adam and myself.

I don't know what therefore made me feel so sad. It was not just my lost sister, surely; or the way the bird, having acknowledged us, went away regardless; or the incomprehension of my slightly jealous husband; not even the story that I'd heard and which Sammael claimed to be my own. Yet I was sad, and because of it, though Adam and I lay all night with our bodies touching, our minds seemed further apart than they had the previous night when I slept alone and far away.

At dawn, beneath the fading stars, the air cool and melancholy, the dew beginning to glitter on the grass, Adam rolled over and still half asleep, began to make love to me. Slow and tender at first, he grew more violent as he awoke, sometimes seizing whole handfuls of my flesh—in either case he never spoke a word and neither did I. But for a long time afterwards he kissed me gently, while I wept silent tears for reasons which I did not understand, but which had more to do with my husband this time than they had to do with Lilith. Once, very tenderly, I found him licking tears from my cheeks. "They taste salt," he said, his first words and his last.

Though the dew had begun to dry outside our bower, the air was still sharp and cool. The sun sifting through it softened it little by little, the same way it took the glitter from the grass. I washed my face and body in the cold dew that remained, shivering as I did so and wondering why I still felt melancholy, and why Adam and I were so quiet and awkward with each other. Patting my shoulder clumsily, avoiding my eyes, he told me almost apologetically that it was time he was off.

"Where to?" I asked listlessly; but he did not answer me.

I felt better as soon as he had gone. The autumnal scents of the early morning, overtaken gradually by the wearier yet more mellow scents of later summer, I found growing in myself a lush, even overblown excitement. Just as I expected upon setting out to look for it, the river had quietened since I last tried to cross. I hesitated when I saw the serpent waiting on the bank, not sure if I desired his company.

After a moment I walked down the bank into the water, too drugged by the scent of the apples to care if he followed me or not. There were so many apples weighing down the branches of the tree that I was wondering how I would choose one—maybe it didn't matter. And maybe if it did, he would be able to advise me. Certainly, my thoughts were all of the apple not the fig—why? I wonder often, when I think about it now. Even then I must have known where my true desire was leading.

Chapter Three

My story's almost done now. And here I remain, empty of desire for Eden, though Adam, my husband, went on hoping to regain that green and fertile place right up till that day, an age ago, that I closed his eyes for him.

I do not know where he went then, death still being denied to me. Any more than I know where Abel went the night he left his body or where Cain did when he went away from me. Sometimes, still, on the other hand, I hear the owl's lonely cries from the desert and know that I am hearing Lilith's voice. As I know that Jehovah is still and forever roaming the empty garden, mourning the step that he goaded us into taking; and that Sammael continues to fall into eternity convinced, for eternity, of his righteous passion, his righteous disobedience.

As for the serpent, Sammael's friend, servant, admirer; I will tell you how once, long ago—Cain must have been four or so and Abel still a baby—we lost our eldest son in the desert for three whole days. And when we discovered him at last, asleep under a thorn bush, filthy dirty, scratched all over, with the tear marks smeared down his grimy face and one foot swollen and red from a thorn he'd trodden on, a snake lay coiled beside him. Just any snake maybe. Yet I do not think I could have mistaken those discreet diamond markings, the faint coppery sheen that I had known so well in Eden; let alone the once melancholy brown eyes now glittering and evil. He raised his head as we approached. Flicking out his tongue and hissing viciously, he defied us to come any further.

Perhaps it was at that moment my love for the serpent became most fully hate—a hate inextricable from fear, it is true, though I suspect that I need not have feared him on Sammael's son's account. But I did not know for sure, knew only my terror and helplessness seeing the flat head sway nearer and nearer the flank of my little son. As the dizzy tongue began licking at his skin, I cried out, I could not help it. The snake stilled at the sound; its head raised, it stared at me as venomously as it had that other time, while I, staring as pitilessly back, agreed our enmity.

Maybe that was all he wanted. For immediately, uncoiling himself, he slithered off, his uncanny, unmoving movements so swift he was out of sight almost before I'd realised his going. Adam, flinging a stone after him, only managed to hit a rock.

Which is the end of it. And brings me back at last to where I began; to what I did and why I did it. I even find myself suspecting sometimes that leaving aside all the other more significant reasons, I ate the fig—the fruit of knowledge—in order to have a story to tell; and in order to know how to tell it, in my own way, before the serpent had time to. Not least because I could learn, I was sure, to tell it better.

But as I've said, you need excuses for action as well as motives and reasons. And what I said right at the beginning was the truth, no more nor less—when I first put the fig to my lips I was pretending to tease the serpent. An unhappy pretence, of course, considering what happened to him thereafter; all my guilt begins and ends with that, as Jehovah no doubt intended. (Was it Sammael said once or the serpent, in one of their interminable discussions, that without guilt Jehovah would be powerless, over us, or anyone?)

Yet I think now that I could not have done what I had to, for the reasons that I did, and looked straight at them all the while. If I'd set out that morning with the clear intention of changing the world—or telling my story of it—I'd never have reached the island, whether the river was running too high for me or not. As it was, the serpent close behind me, the water barely up to my breasts, I waded across carefree, thinking only of the apples.

★

When we stepped up on to the far bank I could not think why my companion was holding out a fig leaf he'd taken from the water, smiling one of his more enigmatic smiles.

"What am I to do with this?" I asked, in astonishment.

"I'm sure you'll find a way to put it to good use," he replied, meanwhile shaking the water from his body with smooth and confident gestures—the drops rolled off him I noticed, leaving no trace behind, whereas I still glittered with water from my shoulders to my feet.

But everything seemed to be glittering that morning. The light by now had shaken off its weariness and beamed with such intensity that every leaf, every fruit, each single blade of grass vibrated light, or reflected light, or else, catching its rays from some other angle, let the light stream through it. I had not believed so much colour was left in the garden—almost mineral colour it was so brilliant, though at the same time fleshy and tender. The red and green of the apples; the muted purple of the figs; the amazingly vivid blades of grass. I noted the passing iridescence of the dragonflies that darted on the far side of the river, above reeds the heads of which also displayed some almost metallic glitters; noted too the intolerable black and gold of the wasps that were burrowing in the apples. At the same time I found myself longing to trace—with my fingers—better still with my tongue—the delicately branching veins on each translucent leaf that threw its shadow or half its shadow on the leaf before or behind it.

As for what I had come for—I could, I thought, have eaten not just the apples but everything I saw. I could have eaten the serpent he was smiling at me so benignly. I could even have eaten the less than delectable figs. Their purple was brighter than it looked, I discovered, when I put out a finger and dusted off the bloom, but still they appeared dull compared to the apples, moreover had no scent so far as I could tell.

Yet their flesh gave substantially beneath my fingers. They too were indubitably ripe. Their softness at odds with the brilliance of the day, I looked quizzically at my friend the serpent, and saw him smiling at me again, though faintly.

"That isn't, is it, the fruit you propose to eat?" he was enquiring.

"Of course not," I replied hastily, turning my back on both him and the tree, to find that the river was as dazzling as the rest, hustling round impediments, giving off gleams and flashes from every eddy—almost the only thing I saw that day which did not try to dazzle me completely was the fig tree, its grey bark and yellowing leaves, its dusty purple fruit.

"Well?" enquired the serpent again. "What are we waiting for? If you are going to eat one of those wretched fruit, Eve, why do not eat it now, then we can take ourselves to some more congenial spot."

He was goading me, I could see. I do not know to this day if he was attempting to bend me to his or another's purpose—it could as easily have been that he was incorrigibly wily, whether he needed to be or not. Nothing that morning had yet been decided; alternatively everything had. In no hurry now that the scent of the apples wafted all round me, I let the day pass at its own pace, considering pleasurably and without urgency the nature of the experience I was about to undertake. What would the apple taste of? How would it feel to be possessed of eternal life?

Yet these were not the questions I went on to ask the serpent. Instead, a brief image of Cain's bloody weapon slipping through my head, I heard myself enquiring in a clear, deliberate voice, "Is it not time you told me about death? Is it not time you told me everything?"

I turned then and faced him directly. His brown eyes seemed veined, today, as brilliant as jewels—yellow, I saw in them, brown and green and red, shifting and changing all the time like the colours at the heart of his furnace. Meanwhile, I noticed, he was licking his lips rather nervously, his tongue darting in and out. His head flatter than usual, his scales more pronounced, he seemed a stranger for a moment; till he spoke, peevishly, in a manner I knew only too well.

"How many times have I told you, Eve," he said, "that it's not a question I can answer, unless you eat that fruit. And it's too late now; you've chosen the other one."

"Not quite," I said. "Not quite." Yet I still thought at that moment I had chosen the apple, not the fig.

"Don't you want to live for ever?" he was asking me.

For ever and for ever and for ever. The words echoed through my head most strangely. They pulled me out among the stars, where, though I loved them, I did not want to be, into an emptiness I feared.

"*Don't* you want to live for ever?" he insisted, with an irritable look.

"If you won't tell me about death," I pleaded, "at least tell me what else lies beyond the garden wall."

The serpent looked at me then more strangely than ever. He hissed to himself so quietly, I was not sure if I actually heard him say what I knew perfectly well, that I had already seen something for myself. If he did, it did not suit me to acknowledge it. Instead I said very briskly, "I'm growing very hungry. But I don't want to eat an apple from the bottom of the tree. Why not climb up and fetch me one from the top?"

Immediately he looked much more cheerful. "How can I resist," he replied, mockingly, "a request so charmingly put?" his mockery belied at once, however, by the affectionate glance we exchanged, by the palpable sense of his relief. Neither of us was afraid any longer. When the serpent climbed up into the tree I followed him, though I don't think I looked as he looked, part of the apple tree. There were no birds in the branches that morning. There never had been birds in either tree, at least I hadn't seen one, and was surprised to discover a deserted nest beneath my hand, made of twigs and lined with feathers.

The serpent was calling down to me now, but I could not hear what he said; how far away he was, I thought—from the ground the tree had never seemed so high. I thought also, for no reason, blinking in the rays of the sun, that today's sharp light must mean that the season was changing—also that such things had never made me feel uneasy before.

"Quick, quick," I shouted up to him, "please bring me down my fruit."

He did not seem to have heard me. All the same in just a minute he had swung himself neatly from the crown of the apple tree into the crown of its neighbour, the fig, which he descended as neatly as he had ascended the other, insinuating himself intimately round its trunk and its branches. The moment I myself jumped down from the apple tree I found him standing beside me, an apple in his right hand, a fig in his left. Regarding me intently, he began to juggle skilfully with them both, splitting the skin of the fig to reveal its fibrous pink interior. Immediately he cast it down into the long grass, reached up and picked another. Yet it was the apple he began holding out to me, saying impatiently, "I can't think why you've still not had a bite, after the trouble I took to fetch it."

At the same time he affected indifference to my decision. But I wasn't indifferent at all. I was wondering why I wasn't digging my teeth through the skin of the delectable fruit, whose smell made me faint with desire.

"Maybe I should wait for Adam after all," I said, my voice prim with uncertainty. "I daresay he'll come round to eating in the end."

"That's just an excuse, Eve," the serpent chided me. "You know as well as I do that the problem is you don't know which fruit to eat."

And I did know. I don't think I imagined the sudden gust of chillier wind. The light too seemed to dim for a moment. Yet immediately it began glittering so brightly again that it might itself have uttered the sharp notes of the bird song from the far side of the river. Light bounced off the apples. Light was absorbed by the figs. If you opened a fig, I wondered, would you find it full of light? A silly thought entirely—I'd already seen the inside of a fig.

"Now it comes to it, I don't care for the idea of eating either," I said very coolly. "How about you? Which one would you choose? Or is the fig forbidden to you also?"

"How should I know?" the serpent shrugged his shoulders, meanwhile giving me a bright and rather shifty look, followed by a dulling of his jewelled eyes, both so swift, however, I could have imagined them.

"Then tell me which fruit you'd like *me* to eat?" I asked. Feeling that I was being crafty now in some guileful game whose purpose he hadn't told me, I was disconcerted by his immediate and matter-of-fact reply.

"The apple of course. What else? Here you are, Eve, take a bite; you know how you've longed to."

So there it was—between willing and unwilling I took the apple from him and held it between my hands. My tongue was actually licking its shiny surface; my teeth preparing to break through its rosy skin—I might even then have been teasing him—was certainly teasing when I paused, snatched the fig from his other hand, and having looked at it for a moment flung it down and picked another.

"Don't," he said, as I held it to my lips, in place of the apple. "Don't, Eve, don't." Nor did I imagine the horror in his eyes, succeeded by bewilderment, succeeded by triumph was it—and then by horror again. Perhaps he didn't know what he wanted of me, any more than I knew at this moment what I wanted of myself. His marvellous golden skin—I could almost catch the movement of his breath in it, rising and falling—was a little too close to me now for his comfort or for mine. Just as in his cave in the mountain, either of us could at that moment have encompassed the other one and in that way changed everything. We did not, we withdrew a little.

I enquired innocently, "Why should I do what you want?" setting my mouth to the ribbed and purple fruit. "Tell me about death," I goaded him, cruelly, allowing my teeth to brush its skin. "That is if you don't want me to eat the fig. Tell me about birth. Tell me if what Sammael said was true. If you do, I'll eat the apple."

Yet at that precise moment, even as I spoke, even as I laughed at him, drawing nearer him to again, as he perceptibly recoiled, my teeth began puncturing the skin of the fig. A childish, accidental act you could say, this eating, in its beginning. Yet the moment that I realised what I did it became a knowledgeable bite, the considered, careful action of a woman who needing, as a woman, what the garden could not give her, had to take the risk that her husband would not follow.

How yielding the fig is compared to the apple, I was thinking, the pink flesh moulding itself to my mouth—it was, after all, my moment of triumph, the moment for which the serpent's skills had prepared me; in which, exercising my own will, I became not only Eve but Lilith, Adam's first wife and his second. The serpent watched me meanwhile with a dulled and weary look—I did not think of him as I tore at the fleshy fibres. Nor did I think of Sammael or Jehovah. Barely even remembering my husband, I thought how sweet the fruit tasted and how strange, and only when I'd swallowed its last threads, its final seeds, started to wonder about tomorrow.

Author's Note

Let me reassure anyone appalled by such treatment of the Bible; my additions and rethinkings are by no means as arbitrary as they might seem. Genesis—in itself contradictory in places if you read it carefully—is only the tip of the iceberg of Jewish creation myth; countless more stories are to be found in the rabbinical sources— ranging from the legends concerning Lilith to Sammael's father- ing of Cain. Some of these stories—Adam's naming of the animals, for instance—have even found their way into Christian myth. To those interested enough to pursue the matter but a little alarmed at the prospect of mining the Talmud, I'd recommend Louis Ginzberg's *Legends of the Jews* (Jewish Publications Society of America, Philadelphia 1909–38—in 7 volumes, I fear, but most of our material is in the first); *Hebrew Myths, The Book of Genesis*, by Robert Graves and Raphael Patai, McGraw Hill, New York 1964, is also helpful, as is Rappoport's *Myths of Ancient Israel*.

As to my attempt to justify Eve; the point has been well made in various studies that the early history of the Hebrews—the Bible itself makes this clear enough—involved a long-term struggle by the monotheistic patriarchal religion that was to become Judaism as we know it, to establish its supremacy over the still lively goddesses of the older mother-worshipping rituals. Raphael Patai's *The Hebrew Goddess* (Philadelphia KTAV, 1976) sets the argument out fully, while Merlin Stone in *The Paradise Papers* (published by Virago, hence the most easily available of the books I've been quoting) takes it on to suggest, very cogently, that the story of Eve and the serpent was deliberately conceived by the Jewish priesthood as propaganda to undermine the role of women and hence of the goddesses and their more polytheistic, orgiastic rites.

Finally, broadening the scope a little, I should like to point out that the Jewish myth of the fall is just one among many. In most mythologies, the coming of death is seen to be inevitable; in the western versions almost alone—Genesis and the story of Pandora, in particular—were the persons who brought it declared culpable, so damned. The treatment of *Eve: Her Story* must make it clear that I tend to prefer the other, more resigned approach (though as Eve herself suggests the issue may not always be so simple). My own collection of creation myths, *Beginnings* (Chatto and Windus 1977) gives various alternatives— and a more extensive bibliography—to anyone wishing to investigate for themselves.

Finally, since I began my account, there has appeared in the USA *Eve The History of an Idea* by J. A. Phillips (Harper & Row, San Francisco, 1984). A comprehensive survey of the mythology, this book has confirmed and classified my intuitions concerning the myth, and may do the same for any reader wishing to pursue it further.